"We've got to move..."

"I'm ready."

There were broken branches and tall, flat rocks to dodge. Lindsey wrenched her ankle on the ninth hole and stumbled, catching herself on one knee. Silver was there again to help her up. He slung his arm around her lower back.

"Put your arm around my shoulders."

Just as they reached cover, their enemy took another shot. A bullet hit nearby.

Silver's more-blue-than-purple gaze punched hers. "You all right?"

He was dripping blood everywhere, and he was worried about a sore ankle? "I can make it to the dorm."

"I could carry you."

Like a sack of Santa's gifts slung over his shoulder? "No, thanks."

"This guy's a good shot," he warned. He wasn't out of breath, like her, but his forehead glistened. "We'll have to move fast."

Lindsey offered a swift prayer for God's protection. At Silver's signal, they burst across the golf course.

And a hail of gunfire followed in their wake...

Karen Kirst was born and raised in East Tennessee near the Great Smoky Mountains. She's a lifelong lover of books, but it wasn't until after college that she had the grand idea to write one herself. Now she divides her time between being a wife, homeschooling mom and romance writer. Her favorite pastimes are reading, visiting tearooms and watching romantic comedies.

Books by Karen Kirst

Love Inspired Suspense

Explosive Reunion
Intensive Care Crisis
Danger in the Deep
Forgotten Secrets
Targeted for Revenge
Smoky Mountain Ambush

Visit the Author Profile page at Harlequin.com for more titles.

SMOKY MOUNTAIN AMBUSH

KAREN KIRST

LOVE INSPIRED SUSPENSE
INSPIRATIONAL ROMANCE

LOVE INSPIRED® SUSPENSE
INSPIRATIONAL ROMANCE

Recycling programs for this product may not exist in your area.

ISBN-13: 978-1-335-55465-9

Smoky Mountain Ambush

Copyright © 2021 by Karen Vyskocil

This edition published by arrangement with Harlequin Books S.A.

For questions and comments about the quality of this book, please contact us at CustomerService@Harlequin.com.

Love Inspired
22 Adelaide St. West, 40th Floor
Toronto, Ontario M5H 4E3, Canada
www.Harlequin.com

Printed in U.S.A.

He that dwelleth in the secret place of the most High
shall abide under the shadow of the Almighty.
I will say of the Lord, He is my refuge and my fortress:
my God; in him will I trust. Thou shalt not be afraid for
the terror by night; nor for the arrow that flieth by day.
—*Psalms* 91:1–2, 5

Acknowledgments

A huge shout-out to Natalie Egeland,
who gave me significant insight into the relationship
between a horse and its owner. Thank you, Natalie,
for indulging my many questions and inviting me
to spend time with you and Chance.

I'd like to thank Sergeant Jeff Duren
of the Hendersonville Mounted Police Unit
for once again helping with this series. Jeff,
I really appreciate your willingness to answer questions
and point me in the right direction. Thank you!

Any mistakes are purely my own.

ONE

Serenity, Tennessee

Mounted police officer Foster "Silver" Williams killed the engine, stepped into the crisp mountain air and surveyed the dilapidated cabins. The waning light cast a pinkish haze over the squat, weathered structures and deepened the shadows in the stagnant woods. Camp Smoky, a recreational property used mostly for church and sports groups, had welcomed thousands of young campers over the years, but those glory days were long past. Why would Lindsey exchange her thriving vacation rental business for this forgotten relic? He'd thought she was satisfied with their working relationship. Happy, even. He put the bulk of his time and energy into his law enforcement career, leaving her to manage his properties. She made reservations, oversaw routine cleaning and maintenance, and handled guest complaints. If an issue arose that Lindsey didn't feel comfortable dealing with alone, she involved him.

Had she felt unappreciated? Had the work become routine? Had she craved a challenge, and that's why she'd chosen to revive the camp? Silver had pored over these questions and more in the two weeks since she quit. His patience had reached its expiration date, and now he wanted answers.

Her red Mini Cooper was parked near the first of six cabins—reserved for staff, if memory served. Perpendicular to those cabins, a long building housed the office, dining area and kitchen. Gravel crunched beneath his police-issue boots. There was a strange fluttering behind his breastbone. Surely, he wasn't nervous? This was *Lindsey*, his capable, conscientious employee, the one who'd swooped into his life eighteen months ago and assumed operation of his side venture as if she had built the business from scratch herself. She was so good at her job that he'd begun to take her presence for granted. He'd assumed she'd always be there to command the ship.

Approaching the cabin, he rubbed at his chest to banish the unsettling sensations. He wasn't nervous. He was worried. Worried he wasn't going to convince her to come back. She could be infuriatingly strong-willed at times.

Scowling at the gaudy snowman wreath covering the top half of the door, Silver rapped on the frame. Everything was quiet inside the one-room cabin. Quiet and dark. Unless she was napping, which he'd never known her to do, she was somewhere else on this sprawling, hundred-acre property.

Silver fired off a text to her number before following the stepping stones around the side of the cabin toward the office. A covered walkway stretched along the back side of the building and connected to the side porch overlooking the distant basketball courts. The windows shone like yellow squares in a brown quilt, and he was sure he'd find her hunched over a desk or fixing a snack in the kitchen.

He was about to step onto the walkway when something in his peripheral vision snagged his attention. The back of his neck prickling, he pivoted toward the patchwork of sickly green-and-brown grass behind the cabins. The sight that greeted him leaked acid into his veins. A woman lay facedown in the grass, motionless, an arrow sticking out of her back. Her brown hair covered her face, but he recognized the cheerful ivory blouse studded with pine trees.

Silver raced to her side and dropped to his knees, ripped off one of his gloves and felt for a pulse. There, weak and rapid, but there.

"I'm here, Lindsey." He started to inspect the wound, but the pounding of feet had him removing his service weapon from his holster.

He ordered the brunette racing toward him to stop. A second later, his brain registered her identity. "Lindsey?"

"Why are you pointing that thing at me?" Her brown eyes blazed at him from behind her glasses. "Help Thea!"

Thea? He glanced down. Lindsey's close friend was also a brunette and about the same size. Before holstering his weapon, he scanned the spindly trees for a sign of the arrow's owner. Seeing no one, he put it away and examined the wound.

"How did this happen?" Lindsey demanded, going on her knees beside him.

"You didn't see anything?" he countered, the terror slowly receding and his customary focus clicking into place.

"I was in the kitchen when I got your text."

Silver contacted Dispatch. Lindsey gingerly pushed the hair off Thea's face. "Thea? Can you hear me?" She bent closer, her features a cloud of worry. "Help is on the way." She turned to him. "Should you pull it out?"

"This is a hunting arrow, and in all likelihood, the arrowhead is a bullet shape. But I'm not about to risk pulling it out and inflicting more damage." The arrow's deep penetration was also keeping blood loss to a minimum.

"Is her unconscious state a good thing?"

"She might've passed out from the pain," he suggested, immediately regretting it. Lindsey's face went as pale as her friend's.

"Has the camp owner given anyone permission to hunt on this property?" he asked.

"Not that I'm aware of."

"Have you had any trespassers? Bored teens looking for something to do?"

"No. It's just been me, the odd repairman and a handful of deer." Her brow creased. "I invited her to come up here. She doesn't like to drive curvy roads, so I offered to pick her up. We were making fried chicken and mashed potatoes. She spilled gravy on her shirt and went to borrow one of mine."

"You're not responsible, Lindsey."

"I—I know. This was an unfortunate accident."

He didn't comment, preferring to reserve judgment until he could get a clearer picture of what had transpired.

"Silver."

Lindsey's big brown eyes locked onto his face. His discarded glove lay in her outstretched palm. He was tempted to dare her to look down, to bare his scarred flesh to her censure and inevitable questions. He'd worn long sleeves and gloves year-round since his teens, to hide the twisted, puckered skin. Rumors swirled around his odd fashion choices, but no one had yet to broach the subject with him.

He snatched the still-warm leather. "Thank you."

He wasn't ready to share his secret with her. Maybe he never would be. His father's abuse had spoiled more than just his skin.

Lindsey Snow refused to let her burning curiosity pull her gaze away from his face. And what a face it was…

Foster "Silver" Williams was as unique as his nickname. The thirty-year-old officer and businessman was like no one else she'd ever met, an intriguing figure with pristine milk-white skin, moonbeam-gray hair, and features that were both elegant and harsh. He was almost always wearing navy, slate gray or black, in or out of uniform. His mesmerizing eyes shifted between purple and blue, depending on his mood, and she often got the feeling he could read her thoughts. Scary proposition, considering she was keeping important information from him.

Thea stirred suddenly, gasping and moaning. "It burns. Get it out!"

Silver reached for her wrist, preventing her from clawing at the arrow. "Try to remain calm, Thea. The paramedics will be here any minute."

Lindscy's heart leaped into her throat. Her friend was suffering, and she couldn't help feeling at fault. Thea continued to thrash about, repeating the same words. Her eyes were glazed, and her complexion splotchy.

"Thea, please." Lindsey stroked her cheek and hair. "You're going to make it worse."

"Did you see who did this to you?" Silver prompted.

She didn't seem to hear the question, let alone understand what he was saying. The paramedics arrived a tortuous fifteen minutes later. Lindsey and Silver waited off to the side as they administered fluids and loaded her onto a gurney.

When Lindsey started for her car, Silver blocked her path. "I know you want to be there for her, but the detective will expect to speak with you."

"Thea is the closest thing I've got to a best friend in Serenity. I'm going."

He grasped her upper arms. "Of course, you'll go. First,

we have to discover who's responsible for her injury and if charges will be brought. We need you for that."

Her gaze was drawn to the retreating ambulance and the pair of official law enforcement cars approaching. "I don't have a choice, do I?"

"The property owner doesn't reside in Tennessee, and you're the sole employee. You can take us through this afternoon's events and provide information that might help us put the puzzle pieces together."

Lindsey understood what they needed from her and didn't like it.

His hands slid lightly down her arms and squeezed her fingers. "She'll likely be taken in for surgery. You would be in a stale waiting room reading out-of-date golfing magazines and drinking terrible coffee."

Silver didn't often initiate physical contact. His leather gloves were supple and soft, but she wished the barrier away.

"And I would be in that waiting room with you, and I happen to despise golf," he added, one gray brow slanting in a familiar, sardonic angle. "Being forced to read about it would be worse than a dentist visit."

He wouldn't be this nice if he knew she'd been sent to East Tennessee to spy on him. He wasn't her true former employer. Her name was on Williams Industrial's payroll, a successful media company owned and operated by Gordon and Astrid Williams—Silver's estranged parents. They'd been monitoring his movements from their home base in Nashville and, when he'd advertised for an administrative assistant, they'd seen an opportunity. Lindsey had scored the position, moved to Serenity and set about making herself indispensable. How could she have guessed she'd start to care about him? That feeding his parents information would make her feel like a criminal? She'd come to a place of such internal conflict and conviction that she'd resigned from both the parents and the son's employ, without giving specific reasons to anyone. Silver deserved answers. She'd sensed God's prompting to confess everything, but she had yet to gather the courage.

"I'll cooperate," she said at last. "After I call Thea's mom."

He nodded and released her, striding away to greet the patrol officer and detective. She could feel their group assessment as she spoke to Thea's mom, Gail, on the phone. The conversation was brief and emotional, and she took a few moments to collect herself before joining the trio.

Silver gestured to the patrol officer. "You already know Officer Bell."

The reserved, dark-headed man attended the same church as she, Silver and the rest of the mounted patrol unit. He'd been at several of the unit cookouts, as well, which were held at their stables each week.

"This is Detective York."

Lindsey had seen the older gentleman around town with his wife. He wasn't a talkative sort, probably because it was his job to notice things and absorb information.

"I didn't see or hear anything useful," she informed him. "I was inside cooking, and I had music playing."

"Why don't you tell me about your day?"

"I'm in charge of the camp's renovations. I spent the morning getting estimates on the most pressing repairs. Thea texted that she was having a tough day. She and her boyfriend recently split, and she's heartbroken over it. I invited her to spend the afternoon and evening with me, and she agreed. I picked her up between one fifteen and one thirty—"

"Which would put you here at what time?"

"About ten minutes after two. I gave her a tour of the

camp. We hung out in my cabin for a while and discussed our holiday plans. We started preparing dinner about a half hour ago." Lindsey had been consumed with this new job the past two weeks. A good thing, because she hadn't had time to dwell on her guilt or how much she missed Silver. It had been good to see Thea. She'd succeeded in getting her friend to smile and laugh and forget her romantic troubles for a short time. "Thea spilled gravy on her shirt, so she went to my cabin to borrow one of mine. The next thing I know, Silver is here and Thea is…"

The image of her friend lying so still and lifeless was a jarring one.

"Have you had any altercations or problems with anyone?"

"No."

The detective gestured to the cabin. "Let's have a look at the scene."

She led them to the grassy spot and almost bent to pick up Thea's discarded shoe. Silver uttered a warning. "Leave that for evidence."

"Oh." Jerking her hand away, she studied their grave faces. "You're assuming Thea was hurt intentionally?"

"We have to be prepared for any scenario," York said.

Officer Bell put on disposable gloves and placed the shoe in an evidence bag. Detective York studied the area with an experienced eye, mentally cataloging the scene.

"You mentioned an ex-boyfriend," he said. "Who ended the relationship?"

"Thea."

"How did he take it?"

"Royce didn't agree with her decision, but he respected it."

Detective York called out to Bell, who'd been slowly

inspecting the tree line and had crouched down. "Find something?"

Bell held the object up for them to see. A second arrow.

York jotted something down in his notebook. "Is Royce a hunter?"

"He's not what I'd call an outdoor enthusiast," Lindsey replied. "Royce isn't behind this. Not only because he's a nice guy, but because he's on the other side of the country and has been for a week."

"I'll have to confirm his alibi." His phone chirped.

While he took the call, Bell brought the arrow over for Silver to inspect. "What do you think?"

"Looks like the one that hit Thea," Silver confirmed, the corners of his mouth turning down. "Careful, there's a substance smeared on the tip."

Bell proceeded to place it in an evidence bag. York ended his conversation.

"Officer Weiland is at the hospital. It's been confirmed that the arrow that hit Thea was tipped with a toxin."

Lindsey shook her head, unwilling to believe what she'd just heard. "That's impossible." Christmas was fifteen days away. The holiday season had infused their cozy mountain town with goodwill and high spirits. Besides, a poison-tipped arrow was medieval.

"They're running tests to learn the type of toxin so they can counteract the effects."

Lindsey massaged her temples against a sudden headache. Her friend had seemed disoriented and confused during the wait for medical help. Had that been due to the poison running through her bloodstream?

"Did Officer Weiland say how she was doing?" Silver asked.

"Only that she's in surgery."

"I don't understand." Lindsey let her arms drop to her sides. "Who would want to hurt Thea?"

Silver angled toward her, his eyes a deep, glittering navy. "The question we should be asking is who would want to hurt you? She emerged from *your* cabin wearing *your* blouse and scarf. When I first rounded that corner, I thought it was you lying there." His throat convulsed. "Thea is only slightly taller than you, and her hair is almost the same length. From a distance, an assailant could've easily mistaken her for you."

TWO

Lindsey wasn't singing along with the Christmas carols spilling through his speakers. She wasn't sharing her thoughts, either. Hunkered down in his passenger seat, her fingers knotted on her lap, she stared out the side window and didn't utter a sound. It unnerved him.

Her personality was as refreshing and inviting as a spring meadow. She was a warm, exuberant woman who could strike up a conversation with anyone, from the delivery man to the grocery-store clerk to a customer sharing the same shopping aisle. That was one of the reasons he'd hired her. Hearthside Rentals required someone who excelled at customer service, who could exude grace under pressure and genuinely care about his guests' experience. He owned forty cabins sprinkled across these mountains, and he couldn't keep up with the paperwork, financials or day-to-day operations. She had a keen attention to detail and the ability to juggle multiple projects at once, which made her perfect for the job. He hadn't counted on the many ways she'd infiltrate his life or how lackluster his days would be without her.

Hearthside Rentals was run out of his home, which meant they were often there at the same time. Almost from the day he hired her, she'd made herself comfortable in his environment.

He missed her off-key singing. Missed her attempts to coax him into eating junk food. Missed how she babied his cornucopia of animals, as if his boa constrictors cared about her attention the same as his wolfhounds.

Silver flicked his air vent closed. He wasn't foolish enough to think he'd formed an attachment to Lindsey Snow. He merely missed the life and joy she injected into his home.

Glancing over, he soaked in her profile. Her rich brown hair, marbled with gold highlights, was stick straight, parted slightly off-center and lopped off at her chin. The frames perched on her pert nose were red, the same hue as her fuzzy Mrs. Claus sweater and light-up ornament necklace.

She turned her head and blinked at him in the semi-darkness.

"Can't you drive any faster?"

"You don't like it when I speed."

Her lips trembled and her eyes became suspiciously bright. He pressed the gas pedal lower to the floor. The Corvette's high-powered engine purred in response.

At the hospital, his closest friend and immediate superior, Sergeant Mason Reed, was waiting with another officer in their unit, Raven Hart, beneath the main-entrance overhang. Raven greeted Lindsey with a hug. The women had become friends earlier this year. The unit had had to work together to protect Mason, his now-wife, Tessa, and toddler daughter, Lily, from Tessa's vengeful brother. Lindsey had helped out in a big way, providing Mom and daughter with clothing, food and everything in between while they took refuge in one of his rental cabins. She'd done it with a smile, too.

The women went inside to find Thea's mom. He hung back with Mason.

"A poison arrow." Mason raked a hand through his tousled brown hair, his eyes and expression troubled. "That shows serious intent and preplanning. We have to explore the possibility that Thea was the actual target."

"While York is holding a magnifying glass to Thea's life, I'll be poking into Lindsey's," Silver said. The more he thought about it, the more he realized how little he knew about her pre-Serenity life. He hadn't asked, and she hadn't volunteered.

"York is taking the second arrow to the sheriff's department for processing," he continued. Serenity didn't have the manpower or budget for a CSI unit of their own. "Maybe we'll get a fingerprint when officers return to Camp Smoky in the morning. I plan to be there."

"I'll be there, too, if you need me," Mason said. "Cruz and Raven can see to the horses."

"I'll text you in the morning."

Each member of the mounted patrol unit was responsible for grooming, feeding and checking his equine partner every morning and evening. All four officers pitched in to keep the stables clean and in good working order. Cruz and Raven used to be part-timers in their unit. They would work with Mason and Silver during the busy tourist season, then rotate back to patrol during the winter months. Thanks to the area's ever-increasing numbers of visitors, they were assigned to mounted patrol full-time. Both he and Mason were grateful.

"Lindsey was subdued," Mason remarked, nodding a greeting to a nurse as she passed by. "How's she handling this?"

"I'll have to get back to you on that, too."

Mason gripped Silver's shoulder, his dark eyes somber.

"We all know how important she is to you. If Lindsey is in trouble, you can count on us to help."

He made it sound like she meant more to him than a valued employee, which was far off the mark. *Former employee, remember?* "She is important to me, but not in the way you're implying."

"When was the last time you hung out with one of your gal pals? Six months? I heard some chatter over at the bowling alley. You've been MIA, and no one knows why."

Silver used to avoid his own company as much as possible. Being around people kept the memories at bay, kept him from dwelling on the past. In Knoxville, his group of friends had been comprised of other officers. Serenity had a different vibe, and he'd found himself mostly in the company of women. It may have appeared that he was playing the field, but he'd been up-front about his decision to stay single. This past spring, he'd had a first-row seat to Mason's and Tessa's near-death experiences. Maintaining a network of acquaintances and friends had become a drain, so he'd retreated from the social whirl, content to focus on keeping Serenity's citizens safe and his cabin guests happy.

"I've been busy."

"That's a lame excuse if I've ever heard one." Mason laughed. "Tessa has her own theory about the reason, and it revolves around Lindsey." He turned and pushed into the hospital lobby, where artificial trees sprinkled with white lights kept the dreariness beyond the large windows at bay.

Silver lengthened his stride to catch up. "She's mistaken."

Tessa was aware of his history and should understand his reasons for avoiding emotional attachments.

In the surgery wing waiting room, Silver's gaze easily found Lindsey in her fuzzy sweater, fitted black pants and ankle boots. Standing near the vending machines, she was consoling Thea's mom while Raven looked on.

His and Mason's arrival netted curious glances. They were in uniform, and that always got people's attention.

Raven approached as Mason went to slide coins in the machine. Unlike him and Mason, she'd changed into civilian clothes before leaving the stables at shift's end. Tall and slender, she oozed an innate confidence and authority that others reacted to—in or out of uniform.

"Thea will be in surgery for at least another hour." Her honey-brown eyes, tipped with thick, sooty lashes, studied him. "Lindsey mentioned in the elevator that you think the arrow was meant for her."

"That's the direction I'm leaning, yes."

"Any idea who might want her dead?"

"Not at the moment."

"This attack coming so soon after she left your employ is suspicious. Did you ever get her to tell you the real reason she left?"

"No."

She cocked her head, and her long, black braid whipped behind her shoulder. "Did you do something to hurt her feelings?"

"No, of course not." At least he didn't think so.

There were too many unanswered questions, a situation he planned to remedy that night. Mason and Raven went home as soon as Thea's doctor gave them an update. Her prognosis was good, barring any infection. They would keep her for several days for observation.

When Thea's mom urged Lindsey to go home and get some rest, she did so reluctantly. Silver escorted her through the building and out into the starry night.

"Stay at my place tonight," he urged. "Take one of the spare bedrooms."

Wistfulness flashed, followed by a grimace. "I appreciate the offer, but I can't."

"If you'd rather not share the same floor as Axel and Ansel," he teased, referencing his boa constrictors, "take the couch in the office."

"I need to stay at the camp."

"It's me you don't want to share the same floor with, isn't it? Afraid my snores will shake the foundation?"

Above her glasses, her brows crashed together. Something like remorse danced over her girlish features. "I'm exhausted, Silver. Either take me to Camp Smoky, or I'll get a ride with someone else."

He stared at her, surprised by her vehemence. Was it fatigue making her snippy? Hunger? Worry about the stranger hunting either her or Thea? Or something else, something he didn't dare unearth. Because his instincts were screaming out a warning. Lindsey was hiding something.

Of course, he did the gentlemanly thing and accompanied her inside the cabin to make sure no danger awaited her. Lindsey's guilty conscience made her stomach ache and her temples throb. She didn't deserve his concern.

Removing the ornament necklace and tossing it on the lopsided table, she jammed her hands on her hips. "I'll be fine. I'll lock the doors and sleep with my phone beside my pillow."

He lounged against the door and crossed his arms. "Be honest with me, Lindsey. Why did you quit? I don't accept that you simply got bored one day and decided you needed a greater challenge." His eyes radiated confusion in his elegant face. "I thought you were happy."

Confess or don't confess? *I know what You want me to do, Lord, but I'm scared.*

Her heart threatened to collapse under the tension. "I was happy."

In the beginning, she'd treated this unusual work assignment as a fact-finding mission. For so long, Silver Williams had been steeped in mystery. As she'd infiltrated his life, she'd reveled in learning the ins and outs of his business and meeting his guests' varying needs. Instead of amassing more wealth for an ambitious, at times ruthless couple, she'd been working to please customers. As time went on, her goals expanded to earning Silver's praise. The mystery faded bit by bit, and Silver became someone she admired. That's when her deception began to chafe. The weekly reports to his parents became more difficult and ultimately, untenable.

He straightened, his arms dropping to his sides. "I'll increase your salary. Give you extra vacation time. No more calling you on the weekends or talking about work at church, I promise."

"You're very generous, but I'm committed to getting Camp Smoky up and running by April. The first group is already scheduled. That's an impossible timeline, considering the extent of repairs, but I'm determined to meet it."

"I'll help you find a replacement."

"No."

His head tilted to the side. Because he styled his thick, glossy gray hair with gel, not a strand was out of place. "What did I do to drive you away? Tell me, and I'll fix it."

The earnestness in his deep voice, at odds with his sardonic drawl, gutted her. "You didn't do anything."

"The wolfhounds are protesting your absence. They refuse to eat. I found a pack of your Peanut Butter M&M's the other day, and I ate them because you weren't there to gloat. The customers refuse to deal with the replacement the temp agency sent over. Did you know he's not a fan of Christmas?"

"You don't like Christmas."

"You make me want to like it."

Why did he have this pull over her? Why did she have to be like the other single women in this town who daydreamed about being the one who broke through to him?

He took a step closer. "Say you'll come back."

Despite his superior height, broad chest and long, sturdy legs, he didn't make her feel small, insignificant or weak by comparison. The blue-black uniform enhanced his unique appeal, the starched, dark fabric complementing his pale hair, milky skin, vivid eyes and full, blush-colored lips.

"The truth is—" Her gaze fell on her Bible, and the prompting she'd been experiencing during her daily devotions resurfaced. Past time to come clean. "I haven't been honest with you," she blurted out before she lost her nerve. "I work for your parents. Or I did, before I resigned. They sent me here."

His head reared back. "No."

"I interned at Williams Industrial during college. After graduation, I was offered a permanent position. I got promoted quickly and found myself working directly for Gordon and Astrid. Gordon has decided to enter the political arena. Due to your estranged relationship, they sent me to test the waters. To see if you might cause trouble somehow. You know, write a tell-all, do the talk-show circuit…"

His nostrils flared, and a muscle in his jaw ticked. A tempest churned in his eyes. But he didn't speak.

"I don't know your history with them," she added, feeling as if she was slowly being suffocated. "Or what they're worried you might reveal. They alluded to certain behaviors on your part, teenage rebellion…"

His expression turned forbidding as he opened and

closed his hands, the leather stretching and giving over his knuckles. "Let me get this straight. You were sent here to ingratiate yourself into my life, make yourself indispensable and pump me for information about my past? To gauge my willingness to reveal their sins?"

Lindsey grimaced. "I know it sounds despicable—"

"It *is* despicable. I trusted you."

"Please, Silver, let me explain—"

"No, let *me* explain," he gritted in a voice that chilled her to the bone.

One by one, he removed the leather gloves and placed them on the table. She watched with growing trepidation as he unbuttoned the long-sleeve uniform shirt, revealing a white, round-necked undershirt. He pulled the uniform free of his waistband and, shrugging it off, tossed it onto the chair. He held his arms out in front of him.

"This is what the esteemed Gordon and Astrid Williams are worried about."

Lindsey kept her gaze glued to his face—a reflection of tragic betrayal.

"Go ahead," he taunted. "Look all you want."

"Silver, I'm so sorry—"

"Do it."

She sank her teeth into her lower lip as she surveyed the network of thin scars crisscrossing his muscular biceps, thick forearms and backs of his hands. She bit her lip until she tasted blood. She wouldn't cry. He'd despise her if she did.

Pivoting, he presented her with his back and lifted the white shirt. The scars were thicker on his back, twisted and uneven flesh that must've been caused by a merciless beating.

Without thinking, Lindsey reached out her hand to comfort him, as if the wounds were fresh. The instant her fingertips contacted his skin, he jerked away.

"I don't understand," she whispered. "Your parents did this to you?"

He snatched up his uniform and gloves. "Go back to Nashville. Tell them I have no desire to unearth the past." He wrenched the door open, and she shivered in the blast of cold air.

She followed on his heels. "Please, wait…"

He halted on the porch's edge, his body rigid, refusing to look at her.

"We're done, Lindsey."

She remained in the open doorway as he stalked to his sports car, slung into the seat and revved the engine. Gravel sprayed as he spun around and drove away. Darkness closed in, and she sank into the ancient rocking chair.

How could she have been oblivious to Gordon and Astrid's true natures? Her stomach rolled and pitched. No wonder Silver had severed ties with them. Now she understood why they'd sent her here under the radar. They were worried he would tell the world what they'd done.

Mired in regret, she poured out her sorrow to God and prayed for another chance to make things right. The bitter cold didn't penetrate. Neither did the isolation. Until car tires rolled over the uneven drive sometime later, and she bolted to her feet.

Had he returned to berate her? Or, less likely, to give her a chance to beg for forgiveness?

Another startling prospect occurred to her. Was there really someone out there who wanted her dead? If so, she was completely alone and unprotected. An easy target.

She was edging toward the cabin door, wishing she had her phone or Taser, when she noticed the lights atop the cruiser. Officer Weiland emerged from the parked vehicle.

"Is there a problem?" she called.

"I'm here at Silver's request. I'll be here until morning watching out for you."

In the midst of his shock and hurt, he'd arranged for a protective detail. He hadn't abandoned her to an unknown threat. That was the kind of man he was—honorable to the core.

Her confession hadn't assuaged her guilty conscience. Knowing what she did now, nothing ever could.

THREE

"Silver?" Something nudged his shoe.

The smell of wood shavings and leather filled his nostrils, and straw scratched his cheek. He forced his prickly lids open. The stall walls surrounded him, and Mason was crouched a few feet away. Raven and Cruz Castillo, the fourth member of their unit, looked on with bafflement and concern.

"Did you sleep here all night?"

Silver groaned and pushed into a sitting position. "I must've dozed off."

His dogs would be wondering where he'd been all night and when he was bringing breakfast. His birds had enough seed mix to last, and his snakes wouldn't need to eat until next week.

"I didn't get a text from you, so I came on in to work," Mason said. "Why aren't you at the camp? Where's Lindsey?"

Her name sent a shock wave through his system, eradicating his need for caffeine to come fully awake. Pushing to his feet, he dusted the bits of debris from his clothing and wished he would've passed the weary night at home instead of coming to the stables. At least he would've been spared this further humiliation.

"She's probably having a video chat with my parents."

What exactly had she told them? His breakfast preferences? Hobbies? The supposed reporters he had on speed dial on the off chance he decided to spill their ugly secrets?

He stalked out of the stall—Raven and Cruz leaping aside to let him pass—going by the other stalls on his way to the break room. They followed in his wake. Mason, Raven and Cruz were more than mere coworkers. They were family. Finding him snoring in a stall wasn't something they'd be willing to overlook.

Silver removed the canister from the overhead cabinet and slammed the door shut. He may not need the jolt of energy, but he went through the motions anyway. He measured out the grounds, filled the machine with water and counted the seconds until the hard questions started.

"What happened last night?"

"How does she know your parents?"

Mason and Cruz spoke at the same time. Silver punched the start button and stared at the ceramic gingerbread-man cookie jar. Last year, Lindsey had cajoled him into making dozens of gingerbread cookies for their guests. Although he'd grumbled about it, he'd wound up enjoying himself. And eating sugar, which he tried to avoid. Had she truly wanted to make their holidays special? Or had she thought spending time with him would soften up his defenses?

"I learned that my devoted ex-assistant wasn't devoted to me or my business. Her loyalties lie with Gordon and Astrid." When no one spoke, he spun to face them. "She was sent here to spy on me."

The three of them exchanged dubious glances. Aside from Tessa, the only people in Serenity whom he'd willingly confided in were standing in this room. They knew why his closet was 90 percent long-sleeve shirts, sweaters and hoodies and why he wore gloves like a Victorian gentleman.

Raven practically vibrated with denial. "I don't believe it."

"Doesn't sound like Lindsey," Mason added.

"That's what Gram said." He'd driven through the deserted mountain roads until the heat of his temper had cooled enough to call the one person in the world who loved him unconditionally…his grandmother.

"Hedda's met Lindsey?"

"No." He hadn't introduced any woman to Gram. There hadn't been a reason to. "Apparently, I talked about her enough over the past eighteen months that Gram felt justified in defending her. She urged me to give her a chance to defend herself."

"You should hear her out," Mason agreed.

"No explanation will justify her actions."

Lindsey's betrayal had created a shock wave of hurt and grief, much like the day he'd found his first dog dead on the side of the road. Knowing the woman's presence in his life was based on deceit made him feel like an idiot. It made him doubt his judgment as a person and a cop. It exposed vulnerabilities he'd spent years dreading and avoiding.

The rich aroma of brewed coffee wrapped around him. He lifted his mug and sipped the bracing liquid. It was bold and plain, unlike those flavored grounds Lindsey insisted on buying.

Mason settled his hand on Silver's shoulder. "You remember how angry and upset I was when Tessa barged back into my life?"

"Of course." Mason had been beside himself when he'd learned of the daughter Tessa had kept secret.

"Believe me—avoiding the issue will only make things worse."

"I'm not thrilled with her, either. She's my friend, and she hid this from me." Raven pushed out an exasperated sigh. "But we have to focus on what we know to be true about Lindsey. She's incredibly kind and warmhearted."

"She puts up with him," Cruz interjected.

Raven rolled her eyes. "You're not helping."

"I've lost count how many times Silver infringed on her time off," Cruz responded. "I didn't hear her complain once."

In hindsight, Silver accepted that he had demanded a lot. Maybe she hadn't complained because the extra time meant more access to his life, he thought darkly.

Mason scrubbed at his barely-there beard. "You have to admit she's fun."

Silver snorted.

"Lindsey injects spontaneity and spirit into your life," he insisted, "which is something you've lacked for a while now."

"Well, now she's out of my life for good, so I'm back to being dull and boring."

"I didn't mean it that way."

Draining the contents, he washed out his mug and set it on the rack to dry. "I'm going out to the paddock."

The unit's six horses spent nights outside in the paddock as long as the weather cooperated. A white slat fence enclosed the spacious acres. Trees lined the entire left boundary, providing precious shade in the searing summers. A few hearty pines were mixed in with the dormant deciduous trees. The mountain slopes rising above the valley had a bluish hue, and the dips and crevices were visible... typical of December. In spring, they would transform into a lush idyll.

The Tennessee Walkers were already waiting near the gate, anticipating their morning routine, which included breakfast, a cathartic grooming session and checkup. His gaze roamed over Scout, Thorn and the others. Where was Lightning? His mount was typically impatient for his next meal.

Mason made a sound deep in his throat. "You've got a visitor."

Beyond the paddock, a secondary road meandered between their property and a neighborhood. He belatedly noticed the cherry-red Mini Cooper parked on the road's shoulder. Lightning wasn't present for his morning meet and greet because he was canoodling with Lindsey on the far side of the enclosure. She raised her head and, after a second's span, offered a limp wave.

He fisted his hands and realized he'd forgotten his gloves in his vehicle. Oh, well, she'd already seen the scars. Knew his shameful secret.

Raven's honey-brown eyes filled with compassion. "You owe this to yourself. Talk to her."

He wasn't a coward. Gordon's first outburst of rage had presented itself when Silver was thirteen. He'd been shaken and frightened out of his mind that first time. But after that, he'd met his punishment with laconic indifference. It had only infuriated his father.

Shoving away the encroaching memories, he entered the paddock and strode across the dry grass. His cream-colored horse, officially known as a cremello, greeted him with a tail swish and pleased whinny, as if to say, *Look who's come to visit.*

"Here to ask about your final paycheck?" he drawled, halting out of reach, the white fence separating them. "Don't worry, you'll get what you're owed."

She licked her lips and swallowed hard. "Thank you for sending Officer Weiland. That was thoughtful of you."

He looked away, summoning the shock and anger he'd

felt last night. Those emotions lingered under the surface, but they'd lost their potency. Now he just felt hurt. Looking at her again, he couldn't help but notice her disheveled hair, rumpled clothes and glasses sitting askew on her nose.

Behind the lenses, her brown eyes were huge and sad, like a forlorn puppy's.

"Just say what you came here to say," he muttered.

The sooner they got this over with, the sooner he could forget about her.

"I want you to know that I never snooped in your private things. I didn't rummage through your closet. I didn't hack into your bank account or emails or attempt to access your phone."

"That makes me feel better." He peered down his nose at her. "Thank you."

She gripped the top slat, her short, red-and-white-candy-cane fingernails pressing into the wood. "I'm sorry I hurt you."

He was good at sniffing out lies. Or at least he'd thought he was… Sincerity oozed from her. He could practically taste her regret, it was so strong. A surge of anger zipped through him.

After all these years and the steps he'd taken to distance himself, his parents still had the power to ruin something good in his life.

"Why did you do it?"

She closed her eyes and sucked in a steadying breath.

"Your parents approached me with an unusual request. Gordon needed to know if you, their estranged only child, were inclined to cause trouble for his campaign. They explained that you had refused to speak to them—" Her gaze dropped to his bare hands, and her lips firmed. "Rightly so, judging by what I now know."

He locked them behind his back. "They offered you a generous bonus?"

"I received my usual salary, plus a bonus."

"In addition to what I'm paying you."

"Yes."

He whistled. "That's a decent incentive. Saving up for a trip around the world? Or do you have your eye on a Christmas-tree farm?"

Two bright spots stained her cheeks. "I owe my parents a lot of money. Because of me, they've taken out a second mortgage and multiple personal loans. They've borrowed from family members and friends. They can't retire until it's all paid."

Another surprise. Lindsey had been strategic with his assets. He'd had the final say, of course, but he hadn't seen anything to indicate she was careless financially. "What was the money for?"

Her flush spread until her entire face was on fire. "I'd prefer not to answer."

"Why would you leave your home? Your family and friends?"

Pushing off the fence, she stared at the ground and dug the toe of her boot in the dirt. "My family isn't in a good place right now. There are five of us, my brothers and sister and I, and things that happened in the past affect us today. A change of scenery sounded like the right solution."

"One that involved poking your nose into my personal life."

Silver was tempted to demand she hand over every communication between her and his parents. Despite everything, he was curious about the problems that had led her here. But he was finished with his parents. He was finished with her, too, so none of it mattered.

"Why did you take the Camp Smoky job after you quit

working for me? You could have returned to Nashville and avoided your family members if you chose."

Her head whipped up. "I like Serenity. I've made friends here. I have a supportive church family." She nudged her glasses into place with a trembling hand. "I—I'd like to think that one day you'll be able to forgive me."

Ah, that sticky issue of forgiveness. He was a believer, a follower of Christ's gospel, thanks to his grandmother's influence. But he hadn't quite managed to wrap his head around forgiving those who willfully hurt him.

"Let me be frank, Lindsey. This town isn't big enough for the both of us. It's clear which one of us has to leave."

This town isn't big enough for the both of us.

Silver's words taunted her throughout the day. The hurt she'd inflicted had lurked beneath his terse questions and rigid stance. He'd looked as rough as she did, with his dust-coated clothes and usually immaculate hair falling into his eyes.

She couldn't make a noble gesture and return the bonus money. She'd already given it to her parents, along with her regular salary from Williams Industrial. Her income from Silver's Hearthside Rentals had been enough to pay for a comfortable apartment, car and immediate needs. Her parents had tried to refuse, arguing that their financial burdens weren't hers to worry about. But everyone in the Snow family knew their current troubles were Lindsey's fault. She was responsible for the accident that had left her twin sister disfigured. If she could climb into a time machine and alter the course of events, she would. But that wasn't possible, and she was left trying to make amends.

In helping her parents, however, she'd betrayed a man she admired, a man she was drawn to like sprinkles to a sugar cookie. She'd aided the villains in his life, and based on his reaction to her final question, he wouldn't get past it. Ever.

He wanted her to leave Serenity.

A stiff wind bustled through the trees and toyed with her scarf. Sinking her hands deeper into the candy-apple-red coat that was a thrift-store find, she watched the repairman descend the ladder propped against the two-story dorm.

"How bad is the damage?"

"The hole where the branch landed isn't too bad, but water has seeped into the attic, which has led to damage to the upper-story ceiling." Warren named his price, which was six hundred bucks lower than the previous quote. His online reviews checked out, and she got a good vibe from him.

"When can you start?"

"I can have my crew up here on Monday."

They agreed she would draw up a contract outlining the terms to be signed before work began. As he climbed into his truck and waved goodbye, she received a text from Officer Bell. He'd been called to assist with a traffic accident and wouldn't get there for another hour or so. He suggested asking Silver or one of the others to guard her. Bell clearly hadn't received the memo that she was no longer a priority for the mounted police officers.

After Silver's dismissal, she'd returned to camp instead of going to the hospital and visiting Thea. She'd been in no frame of mind to encourage her friend.

She'd stayed in her office while the crime scene unit combed through the former staff cabins and the clearing where Thea had been attacked. They'd also scoured the surrounding woods. Their search had yielded little of value. The arrow was still being tested for prints. Detective York had been tied up with another case and promised to follow any leads he got.

The distant call of a coyote raised goose bumps on her skin. The rasp of Warren's truck tires faded, and a daunting stillness descended. No squirrels scampered up tree trunks, no birds danced between branches. Thanks to the fading afternoon light, the camp looked like an old painting with muted colors. Whoever had struck Thea yesterday had chosen this time of day to enact his cruel scheme.

Her fingers closed around the Taser in her pocket. Eugene Butler, the owner, had been more concerned with her safety than with any damage to camp property and had asked if she had protection. She'd never used the Taser, but it gave her a modicum of reassurance.

The sound of a twig snapping reverberated through the camp, and her breathing hitched. She started walking toward the staff cabins at a brisk pace. Why hadn't she thought to ask the repairman to drive her?

Because you don't want to believe anyone hates you enough to kill you, that's why.

Lindsey couldn't think of anyone who fell into that category. Maybe this person thought Thea was her or maybe he was after someone else. Or worse, the victim's identity didn't matter. The crime shows she'd watched with her college roommates came rushing back. What if a serial killer had chosen these mountains as his hunting ground?

Not bothering to stop and take stock of her surroundings, she hurried past the gymnasium and the fields, her palm tight around the Taser.

She was nearing the pool house and bathrooms when a puff of air slid past her cheek and a sharp-tipped arrow buried itself into the wood siding not three feet away. A scream worked its way up her throat. Fear skated over her skin.

Lindsey ripped her hands from her coat pockets and started running. She veered right, running along the pool house and chain-link fence surrounding the pool. Woods loomed ahead.

Was entering them the right choice?

Footsteps pounded behind her. She didn't have time to second-guess her choices, didn't have time to stop for a glance at her pursuer.

She pushed her legs to go faster, blasting past one tree after another, dodging thick and thin ones, ducking beneath branches and leaping over stumps. Could she outrun this guy? Was that his ragged breathing or hers?

A second arrow barely missed her, slicing through a spindly branch and arcing to the ground.

She prayed for stamina to keep going. There was a stitch in her side, and she was growing winded. She prayed for deliverance that seemed impossible.

Pockets of darkness were gathering between the trees. Soon, she wouldn't be able to see enough to keep running without smacking face-first into one. Lindsey made the decision to circle around toward the cafeteria and office. The buildings would provide safety long enough for her to call for help.

The footsteps that had pounded after her became less discernible. Was he tiring?

Up ahead, she made out the strip of gravel that stopped abruptly near the bluff. The overlook and steep drop-off wasn't far from the staff cabins. Hope flowed through her veins.

There hadn't been any more arrows. Maybe he'd only brought a couple. Maybe he'd twisted an ankle.

The maybes stopped when she felt a searing pain. The arrow sliced through her upper arm and continued on its trajectory. Crying out, she slapped her hand over the wound and came away covered in blood.

Don't stop. Don't slow down.

She passed the gravel and continued through the short dry grass, trying not let the pain slow her down. But a serious burning sensation began radiating outward in concentric circles. Then her vision became blurry. She blinked, trying to clear it, and tripped.

Lindsey hit the ground hard. Her lungs screamed for oxygen. Her heart thundered against her ribs. She lay there, trying to gather the strength to get up. Her body refused to cooperate.

Shoving onto her back, she stared up at the bluish-pink sky through a network of gnarled, naked branches. Her thoughts were growing fuzzy. A blessing in a way, because the poison felt like fire ants stinging her from the inside out.

She removed her phone and managed to dial 911. "Need help at Camp Smoky. Near the cabins."

The phone slipped from her fingers, and the dispatcher's voice leaked into the air, sounding like gibberish.

Her lids drifted closed. Unconsciousness almost claimed her.

She heard that ragged breathing again, and the shuffle of feet nearby. Her adversary was there to sink another arrow into her. Or watch as the poison did its job.

Lindsey's last thought was of Silver. She prayed he'd find peace and happiness and remember her with fondness.

FOUR

Sweat coated Silver's skin as he mucked out another stall. Lightning observed him from the next one over.

"Don't judge me," he huffed, stopping for a moment and using the rake handle for support. "You wouldn't want to be idle, either, if you'd had a day like mine."

"Who are you talking to?"

Silver spun around and met Cruz's quizzical gaze. He hadn't heard the other man come in.

He swiped his sleeve across his forehead. "What are you doing here?"

"You weren't at home." He shrugged. "This was my second stop."

"I'm headed there soon." Understanding dawned. "You're checking up on me."

"Want some help?"

Silver shook his head and, exhaustion dogging him, headed out of the stall. "It can wait until morning."

Cruz followed him to the tack room. "The Black Bear Café doesn't close for another hour. Let's get a burger."

"I don't need a babysitter."

"I'm here as a friend."

"Mason didn't task you with checking on me?"

"We share a common concern—" His phone trilled. "Hang on a second."

Silver washed his hands in the deep sink. Turning off the faucet, he heard Cruz's tone change and glanced over. His brown eyes were fixed on Silver, and a frisson of foreboding worked its way down his spine.

Cruz ended the call and ran a hand through his spiky black hair. "You need to get to the hospital."

Had Thea taken a turn for the worse? Had the attempted murderer snuck inside the hospital and struck again?

"Lindsey's been hurt."

Silver digested the information and worked hard to keep his gut-wrenching reaction hidden. "The same attacker?"

"Looks that way."

"How bad is it?"

"Mason didn't say." He gestured to the door. "I'll drive you."

"No need." He ignored the urge to sprint to the nearest exit. Instead, he walked with calm purpose toward the offices and main doors.

"I'll lock up and meet you there."

He didn't look back. "Fine."

Silver had had plenty of practice harnessing his emotions. It was a stretch to keep his worry contained, but he managed. There was no question of his going to check on her. While he was angry with her, he couldn't walk away when she was suffering.

He was intimately acquainted with pain, and he didn't wish it on anyone else, even someone who'd earned his trust and then pierced his heart with a dagger.

The trip between Serenity and the neighboring town consisted of a long, two-lane road with steep curves on either end and a scenic stretch in a picturesque valley. He didn't allow himself to speed, although his pulse was breaking all sorts of laws and adrenaline heightened his reflexes. In the parking lot, he took his time crossing the darkened spaces and entering the same sliding doors he'd passed through the day before. He considered swinging by the cafeteria for coffee, but his limbs were starting to shake from the effort of maintaining a semblance of calm.

The information-desk attendant pointed him to the third floor. There was a slight roaring in his ears as he approached her unguarded door. Why wasn't an officer stationed outside? The room was quite a distance from the nurses' station, in a deserted corner, and the door was slightly ajar. He listened in that open space for a minute and heard nothing but the occasional beep of machines.

Silver eased into the room, immediately struck by the sterile absence of color. The light under the sink cast an oblong swath over the bed. Lindsey appeared to be asleep, her hands resting atop her midsection. The pillow and sheets were white. The hospital gown was white. Against this barren backdrop, her hair formed a fan of espresso strands. As he came to a stop between the bed and the chair, he was struck by how young and defenseless she looked without makeup and her go-to red lipstick. Her mouth had a vulnerable slant to it. Usually, she was smirking at him or teasing him or relaying important business. He'd been too busy trying to anticipate her next words to pay attention to the bow-shaped lips.

He clenched his hands at his sides. Her attractive attributes were nothing to him.

Searching her length, he found no obvious wounds at first. Then he noticed the thickness beneath her right sleeve and gauze peeking out. He lowered himself into the chair. Her eyes shot open, and she fumbled for her glasses in the sheet folds.

"Relax. It's just me."

"Silver?" She pushed the glasses onto her nose, the red frames adding a sense of normalcy to the situation. "I didn't think you'd come."

"If you'd wanted my forgiveness that badly, you could've gotten me a chameleon."

Her face crumpled, and she burst into tears. He bolted to his feet and snagged a box of tissues from the sink counter.

"Should I summon a nurse?" He eyed the IV bag. "Do you need more medicine?"

Busy mopping the moisture from her face, she shook her head. Silver gave her time to recover and then discarded the tissues.

"Please believe that I didn't set out to hurt you," she entreated. "At the time your parents approached me, I was already searching for another position outside Williams Industrial. The glamour of working for one of Nashville's power couples had faded. I'd become dissatisfied." Her neck and face were splotchy, and her eyes bloodshot. "I accepted because I couldn't pass up the opportunity to make reparations to my parents."

He was well aware of the facade Gordon and Astrid cultivated and how convincing it could be. Their reputation was flawless, and they worked hard to maintain it. He couldn't blame Lindsey for being sucked into their pretense when almost everyone else in their circle had been, as well.

"I suppose you're unwilling to divulge what these reparations are for?"

She pressed her lips together. Her eyes begged for understanding.

He understood the power of secrets, how some people would go to great lengths to keep them buried. What he couldn't comprehend was why she'd made their relationship into something beyond boss and employee. If she'd remained remote and professional, her betrayal wouldn't carry the same weight. But she'd become a friend.

He changed the course of the conversation. "What happened at the camp?"

She smoothed her hands over the sheet. "The attack happened after the roof guy left. He must've been concealed on the grounds somewhere, watching us, waiting for his opportunity. I guess he likes to watch his prey. Right before I lost consciousness, I sensed him standing over me. I feared he'd shoot another arrow into me. He must've assumed the poison would do its job since no one was around to administer aid."

Silver turned away and stared at the city's twinkling lights. He couldn't reconcile the Lindsey he'd come to know—someone who'd bake homemade cookies for strangers, volunteer at the local food pantry and cry over suffering animals—with the secrets she'd harbored at his expense. She'd hurt him. His typical response would be to cut her out of his life, like he had his parents. But he couldn't leave her vulnerable to a killer.

"Can you think of anyone who'd want to hurt you?"

"I've gone over this in my mind countless times. Hearthside Rentals has had its share of dissatisfied customers, but none of those pose this kind of risk."

"You are skilled at smoothing ruffled feathers."

"You gave me the freedom and permission to do what it took to make customers happy. Not every employee can say that about their boss."

"For the moment, we can take irate guests off the table. Any other theories come to mind?"

"I can think of only one. Last week, I was exploring camp property and discovered evidence of a dog-fighting ring."

"I heard Dale and Hal Shaw had been charged and are out on bail. I didn't know you were involved."

"I was near the property line bordering the Shaws' place. A woman spotted me and pulled a rifle. I explained who I was and my right to be there. She stormed off, and I returned to my cabin and reported my findings to police."

"They're a rough lot. SPD is well acquainted with them." The Shaw family was likely to hold a grudge.

"You think they'd kill me in retaliation?"

"They don't take kindly to anyone meddling in their affairs."

She swallowed hard. "If I saved the life of even one dog, it was worth it."

The nurse bustled into the room and announced Lindsey was being discharged.

"Doesn't she need to be monitored?" Silver asked.

"She received a minor dose of the plant-based toxin, curare. We administered a counteracting agent, and her vitals look good."

"I've never heard of it."

"It's not harmful if ingested." She handed a stack of papers to Lindsey and glanced at her watch. "Patients encounter problems when it enters the body through a wound or injection."

After she'd relayed instructions for wound care, she whisked herself off to her other patients.

Silver squared his shoulders. "I'm taking you to my place. You shouldn't be alone at the camp, especially not in your weakened state."

She didn't offer a fight. "One night."

Walking into Silver's home was like receiving a hug from a long-lost friend. His private haven was the definition of good taste and comfort. The three-tiered structure was built into the mountainside in a private cove, and the facade was predominately glass framed in timber and stonework. The sloped drive led up to the main entrance, where carved double doors opened into a sleek open-plan kitchen and living area. Honey-hued timber beams overhead offset the seamless modern cabinetry and countertops. Ivory couches were angled to take advantage of the view, which consisted of the sweeping yard and mighty hemlocks marching up the opposite slope. Lamps scattered on wood-and-metal side tables added to the inviting atmosphere.

He flipped a switch, and the space became illuminated with merry white lights. The pine bough she'd placed on the fireplace mantel, the topiaries flanking the exit to the corner balcony, the fluffy pine tree…sparkled like Dollywood's Festival of Lights. Hundreds of lights winked their reflections in the bank of windows. The effect was magical.

The cacophony that greeted their arrival was not. Silver's assortment of macaws and parrots squawked ear-piercing greetings from their cages. She braced as the thunderous clatter of dog paws on the hidden stairs materialized into giant wolfhounds bounding toward her.

Silver issued a sharp command, and Wolf and Annika skidded to a stop, their tongues lolling and chests heaving. Lindsey normally lapped up their attention. Tonight, she had a lingering headache, her skin was tight and itchy and her wound throbbed. She approached the pair, patted their heads and dropped a kiss on each furry head. They leaned into her thighs, which she interpreted as a dog hug.

She closed her eyes and inhaled the scents of dog, pine tree and apple-scented candles. She'd worked here for a year and a half, and she didn't miss her downtown Nashville high-rise office one bit. Silver's home had become as familiar as her own apartment in Serenity. His kitchen felt like her kitchen. His pets felt like her pets. Maybe because she'd made herself comfortable here. Her twin sister, Eve, had accused her of not appreciating boundaries. Her brothers had shared that opinion.

Snatches of today's desperate race through the woods plagued her, as did the memories of her enemy hovering nearby, watching as she lay vulnerable and helpless.

"I need hot chocolate," she announced, turning toward the kitchen.

He was stationed behind the elongated island, a Santa mug on the counter and a packet of hot chocolate in his hand. "Already on it."

She passed between the couch and love seat and slouched onto the first bar stool she came to.

He poured heated milk into the mug and used a mini frother to blend the contents. After he topped it with a giant pile of whipped cream, he carefully scooted it across the quartz countertop.

She cradled the fat mug between her hands, a lump in her throat. "This isn't the way it's supposed to be."

"You wanted marshmallows instead?"

"You're not supposed to wait on me." Lindsey forced her gaze to meet his. "Especially not now that you know I'm an informant."

His features shuttered. "I don't want to discuss it."

"Okay. But you taking me in like this only confirms what I discovered about you. You're a good man, Foster Williams. You didn't deserve to be treated the way Gordon and Astrid treated you. You certainly didn't deserve to have someone invade your privacy—" His eyes had gotten stormier with each word, and she broke off before he tossed her out in the cold.

"You should get some rest." Grabbing a fruit-flavored water, he then guzzled the contents and tossed the empty bottle in a recycling bin. After doling out treats to Wolf and Annika, he asked which she'd prefer—spare bedroom or office couch.

Since he was clearly still displeased with her, she chose the office on the bottom floor, far from his middle-floor master suite.

Lindsey took the Santa mug with her.

"Use the elevator," he said. "I'll get a blanket and pillow and meet you down there."

Wolf and Annika were waiting on her when the door swished open, and she emerged into the back hallway between the storage closet and exercise room. They trotted beside her as she carried her hot chocolate along the hallway. One side was a silvery-green-papered wall, and the other was a collection of interior windows looking into the indoor pool. Reaching the front of the house, she turned left and passed the stairs. The dome lights overhead spilled through the floor-to-ceiling windows, barely illuminating the chairs and planters on the veranda. The yard was a black void, the trees beyond a haven for wildlife. And for a murderous individual with an affinity for arrows? For the first time ever, Lindsey didn't appreciate the connection between indoor and outdoor living. She felt exposed to prying eyes. What if her would-be killer had followed them here—

Silver's boots thudded on the stair treads, and he found her hovering near the exit door at the end, peering out at the night.

Reaching around her, he tested the handle. "It's secure," he told her. "The alarm is activated."

The movement brought him very close, and she got a whiff of his scent—a blend of musky cologne and skin-warmed leather. A frisson of awareness zipped over her sensitive skin. He was taller by a mile and in top physical condition. If wishes could become a reality, he would want more than a professional relationship.

But he was out of her league. He was a sought-after, wealthy bachelor. She didn't have it all together and never had. According to her father, she walked to the beat of her own drum.

He preceded her into the office, dropped the bedding on the swivel chair and propped his gloved hands on his hips. "Is there anything else you need?"

A hug would be nice. Someone to hold me while I vent my fears and frustrations. "No, thank you."

He gave a relieved nod. "I'm going upstairs to change and contact Detective York. He needs to know about your role in the Shaw brothers' arrests." He gestured to Wolf and Annika. "Would you feel better if they slept down here?"

"If you don't mind—"

"It's fine." He gave them each a treat from his pocket and issued a command to stay.

"Good night, Silver."

He closed the door behind him. Lindsey scanned the office and noticed her desk had been rearranged. The temporary employee would've organized the office supplies to suit his needs. It bothered her that someone else would be at the helm of Hearthside Rentals. She'd become invested in the company and wanted to see its success continue. What if he wasn't competent?

Her gaze shifted to the pair of windows on the opposite wall, and she rushed to close the curtains. This place was fortified with an alarm system, and she'd be guarded by one of Serenity's finest and his loyal hounds. Those facts didn't quiet her anxiety. Neither did the pleasure of being in Silver's exceptional home again.

Someone wanted her dead, and she didn't know if he was a complete stranger or familiar to her. Was it someone on the fringes of her life? Or worse, someone close to her?

FIVE

Silver emerged from his bedroom Saturday morning and halted on the second-floor landing. "Rudolph the Red-Nosed Reindeer" was playing softly on the radio, and Lindsey was humming the tune as she moved around upstairs. The smells of cinnamon and cardamom made his stomach growl. He was both hungry and curious, but still he paused.

Things had changed between them. No amount of charming quirkiness could make him forget. Neither could her cooking. Neither could the memory of her wan face and very real apprehension.

A pair of shaggy faces appeared at the top of the stairs. Wolf and Annika regarded him with button brown eyes and lolling tongues. Because he couldn't put off the inevitable, he climbed the polished treads and greeted the dogs first, then his houseguest.

Lindsey was transferring thick triangles from a baking sheet to a platter. Spying him, she walked the length of the island and came around still gripping the spatula. Her smile was off-kilter and her demeanor unsure, both out of sync with her cheerful holiday attire. She wore head-to-toe green. Her blouse had billowy sleeves with fitted bands at the wrists, and her leggings design boasted miniature gingerbread men.

"Good morning. I hope you're hungry. I made pumpkin scones with cinnamon whipped cream."

"I see you made use of the duffel bag you left behind."

Lindsey believed in being prepared, so she'd made a habit of keeping spare clothes on hand. More than once, Wolf and Annika had smeared her clothes with mud after a romp outside.

She lifted a hand to her short, damp hair. "I used the shower in the pool room. I didn't think you'd mind."

Oh, he minded, all right. He minded that she was here, squarely in his life when she had no right to be.

"Something's burning."

"The bacon!" She rushed between the island and the wall of cabinets. Seizing a potholder, she yanked open the oven door and coughed when met with a waft of smoke. She removed the sheet pan and almost upended grease on the floor.

Silver strode to help, but he was too far away. She managed to slap it on the counter. His first thought was that she'd burned herself. But then she placed her palm over her wound.

He switched off the oven. "Let me see."

"I'm sure it's nothing. I lifted my arm too high and the stitches pulled."

"Did you keep it dry in the shower?"

She nodded. "Afterward, I applied a fresh bandage."

He lowered his hand to his side and studied her. Her pupils weren't dilated, and her cheeks held a hint of pink. She'd almost been killed last night. She should be resting, not cooking for him.

"I'll finish up."

Her eyebrows crashed together. "But I—"

"Have a seat, Lindsey."

He injected enough authority that she relented and

trudged to a bar stool opposite. As he retrieved plates and forks, his wolfhounds flanked her. She petted them absently.

"I spoke to Thea this morning. She's getting released later today. I'd like to see her..."

"Lindsey, you're no longer free to go about as you please."

"Couldn't we go after dark? Maybe sneak in her kitchen door?" At his hesitation, she sighed. "I suppose you have other plans. I shouldn't have assumed. I could ask Officer Bell."

The thought of James Bell as Lindsey's protector put a sour taste in his mouth. Bell was a stand-up guy, the kind you'd want watching your back when things went sideways. But he was single and lonely, and he'd hinted his interest in her.

"I don't have plans," he said gruffly. "We'll see how the day plays out. I'm meeting York at the Shaws' place in two hours."

Her chin jutted. "I'm going with you."

Silver's gut reaction was a solid no. If the Shaws were behind the attacks, he didn't want her anywhere near there. But the image of her in that hospital bed made him question the wisdom of leaving her here alone, even with the alarm system. Serving in law enforcement had taught him that criminals didn't act rationally 100 percent of the time. This guy might be so determined to get to Lindsey that he didn't care about tripping an alarm. This cove was a solid fifteen-minute drive from the center of town. Plenty of time to get in, accomplish his goal and get out.

He selected a scone and spooned on a generous helping of whipped cream. Sliding the plate in front of her, he held out a fork. "You can go, but you stay in the vehicle."

She beamed up at him, and his heart skidded sideways.

He turned away, distracting himself with the coffee machine. When she invited him to eat with her, he declined, instead snagging a scone and his coffee and retreating to his bedroom. Of course, Wolf and Annika stayed with her. Traitors.

On the outer edges of the Shaws' property later that morning, Detective York questioned Silver's decision to bring her.

"This is hardly appropriate, Officer Williams." His foggy breath dispersed into white wisps.

"This was the better option."

"She could've waited at the station."

The possibility had crossed his mind. The truth? He hadn't wanted to let her out of his sight. Mason's arrival diverted York's attention, and he dropped the subject. York reminded them of their objective, and they returned to their vehicles.

Silver swung into the driver's seat and angled toward her. "Promise you won't intervene. York's allowed me to be here as a professional courtesy. He can cut me out of this investigation at any time."

"I have no desire to tangle with these people—trust me." She huddled deeper into the puffy black police jacket she'd borrowed from him.

Thanks to the sports car's compact interior, she was seated very close. Her eyes were large and earnest, her hair a soft, dark curtain cupping her jawline. His gaze meandered over her eyebrows—just visible above the red frames—down her nose to her prettily shaped, red-stained mouth. Why was he only now noticing these things about Lindsey? And how could he *stop* noticing? This new awareness of her was distracting and unwelcome.

Giving himself a silent scolding, Silver put the car in gear and navigated the rutted lane. Trash and discarded car parts littered the yard. The box of a house was missing bits of siding, and blue tarps covered the windows. Before he got out, Lindsey gripped his forearm.

"You'll make sure there weren't any dogs left behind, right?"

"Animal control would've cleared them out and attempted to find them adoptive homes."

"The Shaws can get their grubby paws on more, though."

"Not through the regular channels."

She bit her lower lip, and worry crept over her features.

"I can't search their property without a warrant," he added, "but I'll keep my eyes and ears open."

York rapped on the door while he and Mason remained in the yard. Hal Shaw answered their summons and, upon realizing it was the law, released a slew of unsavory phrases. He hovered in the open doorway, arms folded over his disheveled clothing.

"Good morning, Mr. Shaw," York began pleasantly. "You might recognize Officers Williams and Reed. They're with the mounted unit. We would like to ask you a few questions."

"We ain't got no more dogs. You done took 'em all away."

"Hal, I thought I heard men's voices—" A brunette loped around the side of the house. Her eyes narrowed to slits, and her mouth twisted. Corrine Shaw had the look of someone who'd had a hard life. "Why are you harrassin' us again? There's nothin' left to seize."

"This is an unrelated matter, ma'am. You see, there's been some trouble over at Camp Smoky. Two women were attacked, and we need to find the person responsible." As he was talking, Corrine started toward the black Corvette.

"I know that woman." Her nose scrunching, she flung

out her arm. "Hal, that's the one who was nosin' around our property."

Silver and Mason exchanged a look, but before they could take deflective measures, Corrine darted past and threw her body against the passenger door. "You turned us in, didn't you?" She beat on the window with her fist. "Come out and face me, you coward!"

Inside the car, Lindsey flinched and shifted away from the door.

Mason reached Corrine first, taking firm hold of her arm and propelling her away. Silver peered through the window. Lindsey looked unnerved but not in panic mode. He stationed himself beside her door and kept his dominant hand free. His weapon was with him day and night, concealed in any number of the holsters he owned.

York kept Hal confined to the porch, and they all watched as Mason stoically waited for Corrine's screeching to cease.

At long last, she gave up. Mason released her, but not before warning her what awaited if she tried a stunt like that again.

She threw a baleful glare in Lindsey's direction. Silver suspected neither Hal nor Corrine had the patience to hunt for their prey. He wasn't as confident about Hal's wily brother, Dale. Silver kept his peace while York and Mason interviewed husband and wife separately.

When they'd finished, Corinne joined Hal on the porch while the officers convened to share their findings.

"Hal claims he was clearing his mom's blocked chimney all day and into the evening Thursday," York said quietly. "As for last night, he was parked on his couch with a six-pack."

Mason nodded. "Lines up with her story."

"I'll pay Hal's mom a visit," York said.

"Did you ask him where his brother has been lately? Last I heard, Dale moved in with Hal and Corrine after his marriage soured." The department was familiar with Dale. He'd been in and out of trouble since his teens.

York leveled his no-nonsense stare at the couple. "Where can we find Dale?"

Hal's scowl revealed yellowed teeth. "Haven't seen him."

Mason scrubbed at the stubble darkening his jaw. "My guess is he's at the pool hall."

Hal shrugged.

"We done here?" Corrine demanded.

"If you see Dale, tell him we're looking for him."

She tugged her husband inside the house and slammed the door.

York looked at Silver. "You want to swing by The Rusty Nail while I interview Hal's mother?"

Silver agreed for several reasons. He couldn't leave Lindsey alone, yet he didn't relish returning home so early in the day. Lindsey would want to cook for him and care for his animals, and he'd probably let her. She wasn't the kind of woman you could ignore.

Lindsey was glad to watch the Shaw place grow smaller in the rearview mirror.

"That was pleasant," she wisecracked.

Silver flexed and unflexed the hand resting on his thigh, and the leather stretched over his knuckles. "Sorry about that."

"She seemed to have just arrived at the conclusion that I'm the snitch."

"Could be an act."

She studied his profile. The day was overcast, and the milky light caught the pink undertones in his skin. His face and neck were flawless, sleek and strong like a marble bust of a distinguished Victorian gentleman. There was no hint of the destroyed flesh beneath his shirt collar. A dozen questions bubbled up, but she didn't dare give voice to them.

"I can't see either one of them wielding a bow and arrow, and neither can you."

His attention was fixed on the winding road flanked by forest. "It's a stretch," he conceded. "Hal's brother is another story. Dale Shaw is meaner than a copperhead and far more cunning than Hal could hope to be. In fact, the department suspects Dale orchestrated the dog-fighting ring."

"Is he handy with a bow?"

"That's what I'd like to find out." The low-slung, powerful car hugged the mountain roads. His vivid gaze prodded hers. "How are you feeling?"

"Like someone is spoiling my favorite season."

"Lindsey."

"I'm tired." Not the usual tired, either. This was a fatigue that penetrated her muscles and bones and made her joints ache.

"That's it?"

"My eyes hurt, which is weird, and my arm is sore. That's it."

His mouth dipped into a frown. "You should go back to the hospital."

While his concern was reassuring, Lindsey was afraid to hope she'd ever regain Silver's friendship. "No, I shouldn't. I'm fine."

"If it lingers, you won't have a choice." He adjusted the heat to a higher setting. "Dale's our best lead. I need to locate him. Mason's got a lunch date with Tessa and Lily, but I can reach out to Raven or Cruz—"

"I want to stay with you," she blurted. His eyebrows rose a notch. "Where's our first stop?"

"The Rusty Nail. Are you sure you're up to this?"

"Positive."

If there was a silver lining in all this, it was the unforeseen opportunity to try to repair things with him or, at the very least, earn his forgiveness.

The pool hall was located on the far end of Serenity, about a mile from the Great Smoky Mountains National Park entrance. At this time of day, the parking lot was practically empty. Silver had contacted Dispatch and asked for Dale's vehicle-registration information.

"I don't see his truck." Silver parked near the weathered log structure. "Let's talk to the owner."

When she and Silver entered, conversation halted and the one pool game in progress paused. Lindsey recognized one or two faces without knowing their names. Serenity was a small town with a population that swelled from April to October, so it wasn't always easy to identify the locals.

The radio was tuned to a country music station. Lindsey tried not to wrinkle her nose as the smells of stale peanuts, beer and cheap cologne wafted over her.

Silver greeted the bartender. The occupants' attention trailed him to the bar. Although not in uniform, he had an innate air of command. Besides, there were only four mounted police officers in the unit, and a big part of their daily routine was interacting with the community. Everyone who lived in the area for any length of time would've met him. They wouldn't have forgotten him because, in her mind, he was unforgettable.

The owner, a stout woman named Louanne, emerged from the kitchen. She denied seeing Dale in recent days.

"He got into it with Chester Jones last weekend, and I kicked him out," she said. "He's sore at me. Probably won't be back for weeks."

"Any idea where he might hang out until then?"

She named her competition, a spot Lindsey hadn't heard of before. Outside, she asked Silver about it.

"Where's Pal's?"

"On the highway between Serenity and Maryville. You wouldn't notice it from the road. The building's almost completely covered with ivy, and there's no sign."

The ride was completed in silence. Pal's was as unnoticeable as he'd said. The place was only slightly larger than her cabin at Camp Smoky, and she doubted it had seen a thorough cleaning this decade. The owner was less helpful than Louanne. They were almost to the car when a darkheaded young woman darted after them.

"You lookin' for Dale Shaw?"

Silver studied her. "Can you point us in the right direction?"

"Try his ex-wife's place."

He thanked her for the information. After she'd gone inside, he opened Lindsey's door.

"Jilted girlfriend?" she guessed.

"That's what I'm thinking."

Lindsey's stomach rumbled. While the scones had smelled like Christmas on a plate, she'd only managed to eat half of one. Silver's quick retreat and refusal to eat with her had dulled her appetite.

At her request, he pulled into the gas station across the four-lane highway and bought her chips and a soda. He retrieved a water bottle from the cooler he kept in his trunk and chugged half the contents.

"I have to go back to camp," she told him. Hospital staff had found her phone and keys in her coat pocket, but her wallet and ID were still at the cabin.

"You'll need clothes and toiletries to last several days," he stated, getting behind the wheel and heading toward the apartment complex where Dispatch had told him the former Mrs. Dale Shaw resided.

Lindsey was startled by his ready acceptance of her extended presence in his home. As much as she'd like to accept his kindhearted gesture, she couldn't.

"Silver, I have obligations to fulfill. I gave my word to Mr. Butler that Camp Smoky would be ready to receive campers on a set date. We're scheduled to host a basketball tournament and a retreat for widows. I've got companies coming out to give quotes on various repairs. I have to meet with them, compare quotes and customer reviews and get work dates on the calendar. I can't do that from your house."

He mulled that over, clearly unhappy. About her response? Or about the fact that he felt responsible for her and his inherent honorable code demanded he watch out for her?

The two-story complex came into view as they rounded the bend, and he scanned the parking lot. "I don't see his truck."

Together, they walked to the only apartment with a wreath on the door. There was no answer to his summons, and no sounds coming from inside. His phone buzzed, and she could tell from the ensuing conversation that it wasn't good.

He stuffed the phone into his jacket pocket. "That was York. The elder Mrs. Shaw can vouch for Hal's whereabouts on Thursday. He's not responsible for Thea's attack."

She studied his face. "There's more, isn't there?"

"She said Dale was furious about the arrest and his dismantled moneymaker. He vowed he'd get even with you."

Lindsey felt the color drain from her face. "He has motive. Does he have a stash of bows and arrows?"

"Or access to this particular plant toxin? I don't have the answers, but I plan to find out."

A door slammed on the other side of the parking lot, and she flinched.

His expression darkened. "Would you truly be comfortable staying up there alone?"

She bit her lip.

"My days start early at the stables, and I don't have a set finish time. I could spare a night here and there, but Wolf and Annika don't take kindly to being left overnight."

"I don't expect you to be my bodyguard."

"Don't you see? You're going to need one until we find the culprit."

SIX

"Do you mind if we make a pit stop?" Silver asked her. "I'd like to bring Raven and Cruz up to speed on your case."

Lindsey didn't have any objections, although she wasn't sure what to expect from Raven. The unit was like a close-knit family. While they had their fair share of disagreements, they were fiercely devoted to one another. Raven may not be willing to forgive her for hurting Silver.

Silver stopped at Gus's Deli and purchased several sub sandwiches for the group. When he turned off the main highway into their church parking lot, she shot him a questioning glance.

"We aren't going to the stables?"

"They're meeting with the staff about this year's Christmas with Cops."

Lindsey remembered hearing about it last year. There'd been a huge spread in the newspaper and flyers posted around town. Underprivileged kids were paired with police officers and treated to a shopping excursion in the town-square shops. Afterward, they attended a party with food, gifts and games.

Reaching behind her seat, he grabbed the paper sack he'd stowed there. "They're on a break. We'll discuss your case over lunch."

The redbrick building was in the midst of a rolling field. Without the benefit of the sun, the stained glass windows were muted and the silver cross perched atop the steeple a dull gray. Pointed, skinny shrubs concealed the neighborhood adjacent to church property. Fence posts strung with wire kept the farmer's cows from straying into the basketball court. Across the highway, a raft-rental company sat dormant beside the river, the yellow transport vans parked in precise rows until spring.

A breeze trickled through the leafless branches and brushed her skin. She shivered and hurried to catch up with him.

Inside the vestibule, they were met by Pastor Crenshaw. He had heard about Lindsey's attack and assured her that he and the congregation were at her service. His earnest demeanor and compassionate nature had won her over during her first visit. Silver's opinion of the man and his ministry was a mystery. Whenever she broached spiritual matters, he became troubled, and she hadn't pressed.

The pastor returned to his office, and she and Silver navigated a deserted hallway papered with missionary posters and children's drawings. They turned the corner into a smaller, darker hallway. Through the propped-open doors, she spied Cruz strolling toward them.

"I'm starving," he said, rubbing his hands together. "That's not the only bag, I hope. What will you all eat?"

Silver held it out of the other man's reach. "Don't be so greedy."

Cruz made a grab for it, and Silver held it higher still.

Raven trailed on Cruz's heels and rolled her eyes. "Play nice, boys."

Folding tables had been pushed together to form a rectangle in the middle of the bright meeting space. The men chose chairs that faced the door, one of those quirks of military and law enforcement, she supposed.

Raven's perceptive gaze zeroed in on Lindsey, and she steered her to the corner. "How are you feeling today?"

Her cheeks heated. "Miserable for deceiving you. I'm sorry, Raven."

"You already apologized."

"Texts don't count."

"Yours was more like a novel," she noted wryly, cocking her head. Since she was off duty, she'd left her long black hair loose. The shiny strands slid over her shoulder. "I don't condone what you did, but you came clean. That counts for a lot in my book."

"Are we still friends?"

Raven's somber expression lifted, and she squeezed Lindsey's hand. "The question never crossed my mind."

Chatter from another part of the room heralded the arrival of two women who made a beeline to the male officers. Jody Pritchard, a statuesque redhead who managed a clothing boutique, cozied up to Silver. Lindsey's mouth felt full of nails. Seeing him with his adoring fans had always been tough to swallow. Now that she'd given up her place in his life, it was even more heart-wrenching. To his credit, he didn't let the attention go to his head.

"How are things between you and Silver?" Raven asked quietly.

Tearing her gaze away, Lindsey wrestled with regret. "I don't deserve a second chance, but I'm praying he gives me one."

Raven's honey-brown eyes sparkled with speculation. "Lindsey, do you care for him as more than a friend?"

"That would be unwise. I'm nothing like the women he prefers to hang out with."

"It's important to note he hasn't dated any of them."

Tapping her chin, she studied the group at the other end of the room.

"I've wondered about that." Lindsey would be ashamed to admit that the drought in his social life had buoyed her spirits.

"Tessa and I have our theories."

Surely Raven wasn't suggesting he was interested in *her*. "He couldn't possibly— We're from different worlds." Silver may not live on the same extravagant plane as Gordon and Astrid, but her standard of living wasn't anywhere close to his. He'd grown up with a sophisticated crowd, and she was certain that was the type of woman who'd fit his set of requirements in the love department. Take Jody, for instance.

The redheaded beauty and silver-haired officer made a striking couple. Jody resembled a runway model and dressed in the latest style. She wouldn't dream of wearing gingerbread pants. Jody wouldn't supply Silver with hot chocolate or scones. Jody wouldn't belt out carols or roll around on the floor with Wolf and Annika.

Not comfortable with the defeat invading her, she squared her shoulders, only to regret the movement. Her stitches pulled at the tender skin.

"I want to earn his friendship back," she told Raven firmly. "That's it."

Raven challenged her with a single, arched brow. "We'll discuss this later."

There wasn't anything to discuss. Foster "Silver" Williams was out of her league, and she'd be a fool to let her fondness for him feed a desire for more.

After the women had gone, Silver doled out the sub sandwiches. He and Cruz sprawled in their chairs, and Lindsey and Raven took seats at an angle to theirs. As they ate, Raven updated Silver on the Christmas with Cops plans. They had a caterer lined up, someone to don a Santa costume and a team of volunteers to assemble stockings.

Cruz crumpled his wrapper into a ball and tossed it in the wastebasket. "You haven't located Dale Shaw?"

Silver finished off his sandwich, wiped a napkin over his mouth and placed his garbage in the empty sack. "We've got a BOLO out. Can't get a warrant unless I establish he had access to the toxin or owns bows and arrows."

"Talk to the officers who raided the Shaw property. Maybe one of them saw something." Cruz's piercing eyes switched to Lindsey. "Is there anyone besides Dale Shaw with a grudge against you?"

"No one comes to mind."

"You've dealt with a lot of tourists coming through the area," Raven said between bites. "Have any altercations with any? Made anyone angry?"

Silver's head lifted, and his watchful gaze found hers. He was dressed in layers of black.

"There've been some unhappy customers," she said. "That's unavoidable. But no one angry enough to kill me."

Raven peered into her chip bag and scowled. "You wouldn't believe what people kill over these days."

Cruz folded his arms across his chest, brought his chair down to all four legs and twisted toward Silver. "We have to consider this from all angles. Lindsey has spent the last year and a half close to you. Maybe that made someone jealous."

Silver's brows hit his hairline. "You're joking."

"Do I look like I'm joking?"

"He has a valid point," Raven said. "I hope he's wrong, because the suspect pool would be enormous."

Silver shook his head in disgust. "I'm a confirmed bachelor. Everyone knows it."

"Some women might take that as a challenge."

"Everyone also knows that the idea of Silver and I is ludicrous," Lindsey stated, and immediately wished she hadn't.

The three officers' gazes swung to her.

"Why is that?" Cruz challenged, his expression puzzled. "Are you in a relationship?"

"No. I mean… It's just that…" Her cheeks were hot enough to fry an egg on, and she looked everywhere except for at Silver.

Raven swooped in and rescued her. "I think what she meant to say is that their relationship is strictly professional."

Lindsey's phone buzzed and, grateful for the distraction, she read the text. "I'm supposed to meet with Norman Miller on Monday to discuss the footbridge repairs." The bridge that led to the bluff overlook needed several boards replaced. Plus, she wanted reassurances the entire structure was sound. "He's asking if I can meet today."

She reluctantly sought Silver's gaze. He was as inscrutable as ever. "We're headed up there anyway to retrieve some of your belongings. Tell him yes."

She finished her sandwich without tasting it. As they prepared to leave, Raven pulled her aside. "Keep me updated. I want to help in any way I can."

Lindsey nodded, thanking God for friends who loved her despite her flaws.

"Don't give up on Silver, okay? He's angry right now, but he'll come around. You're good for him, Lindsey. He needs you in his life."

Silver didn't like being out in the open when there was a murderous suspect on the loose. While Norman Miller was inspecting the footbridge and chatting up Lindsey, Silver scrutinized the woods, the bluff and the staff cabins, which

were distant shapes at the far end of the meandering gravel
drive. His attention kept being drawn back to the handy-
man. A transplant from Rhode Island, Norman hadn't had
any run-ins with the law. All Silver knew about him was
that he was divorced and eked out a living doing odd jobs.

Norman was clearly impressed with Lindsey. His friend-
liness went beyond the desire to make a good impression
and net a paying job. Silver watched the pair, his scowl
deepening. If Norman put his hand on her back one more
time—

But Lindsey could handle herself. Polite smile fixed in
place, she shifted out of reach and maintained a professional air. "How long will the repairs take?"

Norman tugged on his earlobe. "About a week." His gaze
lingered on Lindsey's face. "Maybe longer."

"Why don't you send me a detailed price quote, and I'll
run it by Mr. Butler for final approval?"

"I'll bring it out tomorrow. Will you be here?"

"That's not necessary. I'll give you my email address."

Norman's shoulders slumped, and he took his time saying goodbye. Silver waited until he was out of sight to
speak. "You don't need the owner's approval, do you?"

"Not on the small jobs."

"I'd like a list of all the people who've come here since
you've taken this assignment."

"Their contact info is in the office." She started down
the path, her hands shoved deep into her jacket pockets and
boots scuffing against the dry grass. Her other jacket had
been ruined by the arrow, and she'd located a backup in
the cabin. "I don't know any of them on a personal level."

He fell into step beside her. "How many are we looking at?"

"At least a dozen."

"I'm not ruling out Dale, but it's worth looking into the

people who are familiar with the camp's layout and know you're alone. Did Norman tell you why he changed the meeting to today?"

"No, he didn't." There was a hitch in her voice. "You suspect him?"

"I don't know enough about him to make a judgment call."

"He seems harmless to me. A lonely man craving companionship."

"You of all people should know appearances can be deceiving," he said with heat.

She flushed to the roots of her hair, and he regretted the dig. Being here so soon after her attack couldn't be easy.

He softened his tone. "You're not the only one blinded by my parents' glittering personas. They're pros at protecting their image. No one would've imagined we were anything other than the perfect family."

"No one suspected?"

"If they did, I didn't hear about it."

"Your mother didn't intervene?"

"No."

"I don't understand her." Her eyes blazed behind the frames. "At one time, I admired her drive, her grand vision for the company, her ability to handle any social situation with poise. Knowing what I know now, I no longer respect her."

"I've come to the conclusion that, deep down, my mother is intimidated by my father. She's allowed him to manipulate her thoughts and actions."

"That doesn't excuse her."

"My grandmother would've taken me out of their home if she'd known. She didn't live nearby, and my father had ways of making sure I kept my mouth shut during our visits." Gordon had threatened to turn the whip on Astrid.

Despite Silver's complicated feelings for his mother, he wouldn't have done anything to put her in danger. "Hedda didn't learn of the abuse until I moved in with her after high school graduation."

He'd told her he wore gloves to mimic a comic book hero, and she'd believed he was in a strange teenage phase.

Lindsey slipped her hand into his. Thanks to his leather gloves, he couldn't say if her skin was soft or her palms smooth. He could feel residual warmth and the slight pressure of her hand. Silver glanced down at her uplifted face, the charming features wreathed in sadness, and his heart pinched with unidentified emotion. He wished she hadn't agreed to his parents' scheme, wished she hadn't worked for him under false pretenses, wished he hadn't let down his guard with her. Lindsey had become part of his exclusive inner circle. She didn't realize that, though.

"If I could change your past and gift you a normal, happy upbringing, I would."

His heart beat in an uncomfortably fast pace. "According to my grandmother, God allowed my suffering for a reason."

Her expression clouded, and she released his hand. "Life's trials can bring us closer to Him," she said carefully. "One thing I do know—God loves us and desires a personal relationship with us. He can use bad situations to drive us to His side."

Silver hadn't become a believer until his college years. He credited his grandmother with helping him find his faith. There were unresolved issues, however, ones he didn't know how to fix.

"It's my job to uphold the law and see that justice is served. I can't understand why my parents continue to enjoy prosperity. They haven't been held accountable for their actions."

Why hadn't God made them pay?

"You could come forward with your story," she said, her gaze assessing. "Do exactly what they fear you'll do."

"Not going to happen." Dredging up those memories would expose his pain and humiliation to the world. He wouldn't willingly take on the role of victim again.

"Then you have to let it go. You have to ask God to help you work through all the messy stuff and reach a place of healing and forgiveness. You have to let Him handle your parents."

His gut clenched. "I'm supposed to forgive someone who isn't sorry."

Lindsey at least regretted her deception and longed for restoration. His parents hadn't admitted they'd wronged him and probably wouldn't, because they would always put themselves first.

"Holding on to rage and bitterness will destroy you, Silver. I've seen it happen. You may think forgiving your parents is unattainable, but nothing is impossible with God."

SEVEN

Silver wasn't comfortable discussing his parents, his past or spiritual roadblocks. Putting a swift end to the conversation, he ushered her to the cabin. She'd managed to sprinkle her special blend of holiday magic during the brief time she'd spent there. He hadn't visited her apartment and being in her private living space made him antsy. He fought the urge to flee while she stuffed clothing and necessities into a bright green duffel.

His gaze touched on the bed's reindeer-print blanket, the stack of books on the bedside table, the tangle of necklaces hanging from a plastic hook and a pine-scented candle. Lindsey's environment—though a bit haphazard—invited guests to breathe and relax, to leave cares at the door and simply be. His grandmother's home had been like that, too. As a child, he'd lived for visits to Hedda's. His childhood home had resembled a museum. He'd been expected to keep his bedroom spotless. There was no joy, no childish exuberance in the Williamses' home.

He'd love to pose one burning question to Gordon and Astrid—why have a child? They obviously hadn't wanted him.

"Where are those pants?" Crouched before a rickety

chest of drawers, she opened and closed the drawers, digging in the contents and muttering to herself.

With each slam, a framed photograph shuddered toward the edge. He grabbed it just before it went crashing to the floor. She thanked him and whirled to the bathroom.

"I'm almost done," she called.

He seized the chance to study the faded picture. Her family, he guessed. She'd shared occasional tidbits about her parents. Charles Snow was a welder by trade. Her mother, Lea, had worked odd jobs through the years to help support the family. The eldest brother, Trent, was a jeweler, Silver recalled. He'd forgotten the other two brothers' names. He brought the picture closer to inspect the twin girls. Neither had glasses, but he was pretty sure the one sticking out her tongue was Lindsey.

"Your sister's name is Eve, right? What does she do?"

The rattling around in the bathroom stopped. "Eve switches jobs a lot," she answered.

He carried the frame to the open door and found her contemplating her reflection in the mirror. Was it strange having an identical twin? Silver thought it might be unsettling to date one. He wasn't sure how he felt about another woman sharing Lindsey's features and mannerisms. In his mind, she was one of a kind.

"Is there a reason for that?"

Her hands braced on the sink edge, she turned her head. "It's not drugs or alcohol."

That had been his first thought. "She gets bored easily? Doesn't get along with coworkers?"

"Eve hasn't found anything that suits her long-term."

He studied her expression, which was much too schooled to be natural. "Why hasn't your family visited you since you moved?"

"My parents wanted to come, but Dad was reluctant to

take off work. In fact, I can't remember the last time they took a vacation." She brushed past him, and her scent enveloped him…something pleasant and simple. Vanilla, maybe. "Not everyone has unlimited resources at their disposal."

She was hiding something. He didn't press the issue because she was clearly exhausted. He would revisit it later. For now, he was going to take her home and make sure she rested.

"Got everything you need?"

Untangling a lock of hair from her dangly earring, she scanned the interior. "For a couple of days. I appreciate your protection, Silver."

"But you have a deadline to meet."

"Exactly."

"You can't meet it if you're dead."

She blanched, and her knuckles went white where she gripped the duffel strap. "You know, most of the time I appreciate your plain speaking. Now is not that time."

"Naivete will get you killed, Lindsey."

Her eyes got shiny, broadcasting impending waterworks. He'd seen victims cry before. This was different. This was his capable, glass-half-full assistant who saw the world as a place of promise and beauty.

He scrambled to stem the tide. "I don't feel like cooking supper, and I'm sure you don't, either." Taking hold of her duffel, he hefted it off the bed. "Why don't we order takeout from Terry's Tacos? You can get those fish tacos you like so much. I'll even spring for tres leches cake."

She sniffled a little. Thumbed up her glasses and swiped at her eyes. "I'm in the mood for flan."

"Done."

He exited the cabin first and took stock of their surroundings. There was no sign of unwanted company. After Silver stowed the duffel, her pillow and blanket into the trunk of his car, they walked toward the office to retrieve the repairmen's names.

Halfway between the car and the building, a rifle blast greeted his ears.

Lindsey didn't know what to think when Silver seized her hand and tugged her close. "Take cover!"

A blast ricocheted through the mountains, and she realized what was happening. Her enemy had switched from arrows to bullets. She would've remained in one spot, a perfect target, if not for Silver.

He held tightly to her hand and pulled her to the corner of the cafeteria. When a bullet shattered the window near their heads, he urged her across the gravel drive and shielded her while she crawled between the fence slats that enclosed the recreation circle.

As soon as he was clear of the fence, they raced over uneven rock pathways and ducked behind the snack building.

"Call 911." He removed a compact black gun from his holster.

She was dialing when he peered around the corner and wood splintered into a dozen pieces. He flinched. Her phone slipped to the ground.

Blood dripped from the crest of his sharp cheekbone to his jawline.

She gasped and reached for him.

"I'm fine." Returning her phone to her, he said, "Stay put. I'm going around the other side."

As soon as he was out of sight, she contacted Dispatch and explained their predicament.

She jerked when two successive shots sounded nearby.

He pounded around the corner and shook his head. "I

missed. He's keeping himself well concealed. You summoned help?"

"She wasn't happy I ended the call." Lindsey couldn't relay events while simultaneously trying to stay alive.

His features were grim, almost daunting. The bright red blood against his bone-white complexion didn't help. "We've got to move." He helped her to her feet. "Let's get to that dorm."

A mini golf course, fence, gravel drive and wide strip of grass stood between this hut and the dorm. But there were trees that could provide cover.

"I'm ready."

Fingers entwined, they darted away from the hut and jumped off a large rock to the tattered golfing strip below. There were broken branches and tall, flat rocks to dodge. She wrenched her ankle on the ninth hole and stumbled, catching herself on one knee. Silver was there again to help her up. He slung his arm around her lower back.

"Put your arm around my shoulders."

He propelled her toward a shoulder-high windmill on the next hole. Just as they reached it, their enemy took another shot. A bullet hit a blade, and the mechanism spun wildly.

They hunched together behind the slim structure. Silver's more-blue-than-purple gaze punched hers. "You all right?"

He was dripping blood everywhere, and he was worried about a sore ankle? "I can make it to the dorm."

"I could carry you."

Like a sack of Santa's gifts slung over his shoulder? "No, thanks."

"This guy's a good shot," he warned. He wasn't out of breath, like her, but his forehead glistened. "We'll have to move fast."

Lindsey offered a swift prayer for God's protection. At Silver's signal, they burst across the golf course. A hail of gunfire followed in their wake. Adrenaline and the officer at her side bolstered her to the goal ahead.

The boxlike structure was the oldest dorm on the property and in the worst shape. During her inspection, she'd taken one step inside and thought better of entering, certain it would need to be razed. She and Silver ran along the crumbling cement wall and around to the back. His weapon in one hand, he turned toward the shooter's direction and pressed close to the building. A moan rumbled in his chest as he jerked back and looked down.

"What is it?" Lindsey demanded. "Have you been shot?"

He scowled at his upheld arm. "Skewered by a nail."

She gasped when she glimpsed the torn jacket material and jagged wound beneath.

"Watch yourself," he warned, gesturing to the pointy nail poking out of the wall near the window.

He returned to the corner and waited for a clear shot. Cold emanated from the cement blocks, seeping into her body. She began to shiver. Minutes passed, and Lindsey's nerves stretched to a breaking point. Was her frantic heartbeat masking her enemy's impending footsteps? She stayed close to Silver, her focus on the opposite corner, anticipating a surprise assault.

Daylight was dwindling. The camp was a vista of black silhouettes against a brilliant orange sky. In a short while, they'd lose their ability to see.

"Should we go into the woods?" she whispered.

He didn't take his gaze off the recreational area. "It's not a good option. No food, water. Overnight temps."

"Hungry bears."

He considered the terrain. "We could use the trees for

cover and travel parallel to the camp. Make our way to the main road."

"I'm all for putting distance between us and his firearm."

Decision made, they entered the woods and walked in the direction of the camp entrance. Through the branches, she saw snatches of the camp structures, and it reassured her to know they weren't wandering into deep forest. On the other hand, it would be easier for their pursuer to find them.

Silver's purposeful stride didn't falter. While grateful for his presence, she worried about the injuries he'd sustained. He didn't deserve to be hurt because of her. Losing him because of her idiotic actions was one thing. Losing him completely wasn't something she could bear to think about.

They reached open farmland as darkness began to edge out the light. A red barn and chicken coop were the only things she could make out in the distance.

"What now?" She glanced behind her, barely able to distinguish one tree from another. "Why haven't I heard sirens?"

"SPD could be dealing with an emergency and can't spare resources. How's your ankle?"

"Not bad."

He frowned and took her hand. "Let's find a place to hunker down and wait for backup."

They walked through short, crisp grass across level terrain. By the time they reached the red structure, she was winded and coated in a fine sheen of sweat, despite the cold. The ache in her ankle was inconvenient but not unbearable.

Behind them, the gloom shrouded the woods and field they'd just crossed. Had their pursuer given up?

As they passed between the barn and chicken coop, the smells of hay, grain and manure greeted them.

"Farmhouse is dark, and there aren't any vehicles in the drive." He pushed open the barn door. "This is where we wait."

EIGHT

Silver closed the heavy door behind him, and the darkness was complete. Lindsey clamped on to his arm. "Aren't you going to light a lamp?"

"Probably not a good idea."

She sidled close enough for his senses to register her body heat. "What if there are critters in here?"

Any minute now, she might launch herself into his arms. He flashed his phone light around. "There's nothing else in here besides us."

"That we can see, you mean."

He couldn't argue with that. He led her to a couple of square bales in the corner and would've turned off the light, but she snatched his hand. "Silver, you're leaving a trail of blood behind you. We have to tend your wound."

His arm was starting to throb in time with his heartbeat, and the way Lindsey had reacted to the gash on his face made him wonder if he'd have another scar to add to his collection...one that couldn't be hidden.

Lighting a lamp was a risk. A small one, as there were no windows and no obvious gaps in the walls. It would also free up their hands so they could work on his wound without having to juggle the phone.

"Shine my phone so I can find a lamp."

He lit the first one he found and hung it from a post peg. The light illuminated the small loft piled high with hay. He shucked off his jacket, unable to prevent a hiss of indrawn air.

Lindsey gingerly peeled back his tattered shirtsleeve. "You need to see a doctor."

Doctor visits were uncomfortable. They would want to know how he got the scars and why they weren't listed in his medical history.

"I've got a first-aid kit at home." Although he wasn't able to get a good look at the injury, he could tell the nail had missed major arteries.

He fished his knife out of his boot.

"Use my jacket," she offered.

"No use destroying yours when mine's already headed for the garbage."

Silver made quick work of ripping strips. Lindsey wrapped them around his lower arm and tucked in the ends.

She knuckled her glasses to the bridge of her nose. "That's the best I can do. If I had my purse with me, I could at least offer you pain reliever."

"I'll manage." He wasn't expecting her to go on her tiptoes and bring her face close to his. His stomach fell to his toes. "Uh, Lindsey?"

Her brows quirked. "I'm not going to kiss you, you big lug. I'm trying to check your facial laceration."

The tips of his ears burned. "I know that."

His mind skimmed over her adamant vow that they could never be a couple. Why was the prospect repulsive to her? She was one of the few people who'd seen his marred body. It was enough to repulse those with the strongest constitutions.

But she hadn't shied away from him. She'd reached out in empathy.

"There's too much dried blood. Without fresh water and supplies, I can't see how deep it is." She hobbled to the corner, sank onto the bale and wrapped her arms around herself. "I'm firing you."

"Excuse me?"

"You can't be my bodyguard, Silver. If you'd gotten shot tonight..." A shudder ripped through her. "It's too dangerous."

He sank onto the hay beside her, surprised by the urge to tuck her against his side.

She hunched forward. "Sometimes I ask myself if I had a chance to redo the past, would I have had a different answer for your parents?"

He studied her profile. "And?"

She blew out an unsteady breath. "I'm not sure."

"I see."

"Does that make me a terrible person? If I hadn't agreed to their scheme, I would never have met you." She turned to him in entreaty. "My life would be poorer without you in it."

The admission surprised him. Lindsey hadn't ventured into the personal feelings realm. Silver had had to dodge Serenity's marriage-minded females, so her professional approach had been a relief. Her complete lack of interest in him had paved the way for a friendship to form. That was why her betrayal had cut so deeply. It was also why he was willing to set his hurt feelings aside in order to keep her safe.

"You can't fire me, you know," he said. "I'm a volunteer."

Her eyes were big and soft. She lifted her hand toward his face. He went utterly still, his eyes whispering closed when she trailed trembling fingertips along his cheek.

"You amaze me, Foster Williams. You came through

your ordeal with your heart intact. They didn't destroy you or diminish your ability to care about others."

Goose bumps skittered over his skin, and he almost captured her hand and held it in place. Instead, he didn't move. He didn't speak.

She lowered her hand to her lap and sighed. He stood and walked to the post on unsteady legs, keeping his back to her.

"You paint a nice picture of me, but it's not entirely accurate."

His heart was as damaged as his skin. Mason once suggested Silver's issues with his father had bled into his relationship with God and that he'd projected Gordon's shortcomings onto his Heavenly Father. Lindsey's encouragement to find healing had shed light on the root of his problem. He'd granted God access to everything in his life—his career, friendships, finances—except for his twisted past and fractured family.

He scraped his boot over the straw-dusted earth. The lantern's light didn't fully penetrate every corner of the barn. Parts of himself were still locked in denial, the shock and shame he'd endured as a kid. "Parents are supposed to protect their children, not hurt them."

"Is that why you became a police officer? To protect those who can't defend themselves?"

He recalled that volatile summer after high school. "I wanted to make my grandmother proud."

"Hedda thought you should become an officer?"

He pivoted to face her. "I told you I went to live with her after graduation. Finally out from beneath my father's thumb, I went a little wild. I channeled years of rage into partying and drinking. I ran with a rough crowd, mostly older guys who flouted the law. We never backed down from a fight, and I came home multiple times sporting black eyes and a busted lip. My grandmother was disappointed, as you might imagine. Although it killed me to hurt her, I kept repeating the cycle. Toward the end of the summer, after one really bad fight, she sat me down and gave me a stern lecture. I don't remember everything that was said, but one thing will always stand out. *Foster, we only get one life. Are you going to spend yours hurting others? Or helping them?*"

"You're fortunate to have her in your corner." Her voice was husky with emotion.

"I'm not sure where I would've ended up without her. I lost the bad influences, enrolled in college and earned my criminal-justice degree. Then I went to the police academy and earned a spot with the Knoxville PD."

"How did you meet Mason?"

"Our departments took part in fundraisers, including ball games where we faced off against each other. One night, a young girl got injured at the ballpark, and Mason and I were the first to reach her. We stayed with her until EMS arrived on scene, and I hitched a ride to the hospital with Mason. We passed the hours swapping anecdotes. After that, we hung out occasionally. Then he switched to mounted patrol, and he eventually invited me to apply."

That was the best decision he'd ever made. Mason, Raven and Cruz had become his adopted family. Mason's new wife, Tessa, and their daughter, Lily, had expanded the circle.

There was a grunt, the sound of shuffled steps and the barn door scraped open. At the sight of a rifle pointed their direction, Silver shoved Lindsey behind him and reached for his weapon.

"You're on private property," the gun owner snarled. "Didn't you see the warning signs I posted?"

The heavyset elderly man in stained overalls was obviously not their suspect.

Lindsey ducked beneath Silver's arm. "Don't shoot! We're not here to harm you or your animals. Someone was shooting at us, and your barn provided the quickest solution." His rheumy eyes didn't so much as blink, and his finger continued to hover over the trigger. "I'm Lindsey Snow. I'm fixing up the camp. You know the owner, Eugene Butler, I'm sure."

"Get behind me, Lindsey," Silver said through gritted teeth. She halfway obliged his *request*, taking a spot at his shoulder. "Sir, I'm Officer Foster Williams with the Serenity Mounted Police." At the whir of high-pitched sirens zooming past the farm, he said, "The authorities are here at our summons. Lower your weapon, and I'll show you my credentials."

"You don't look like a cop to me," he said.

"I get that a lot. Probably the gray hair. People think I dye it, but it's 100 percent natural. My grandmother and mother both grayed early."

"Hmmph."

"I noticed you have a Percheron horse." Silver launched into a casual discourse about the unit horses, how they were all Tennessee Walkers and had temperaments suited to the rigors of police training and job performance. This disarmed the farmer, figuratively and literally. Inch by inch, he lowered the rifle. He became fully engaged in the conversation and seemingly forgot his ire at finding two strangers in his barn.

In a matter of minutes, Silver had built a tentative connection. The men left the barn comparing the merits of sweet feed versus pellets. Lindsey trailed in their wake, a little awed.

Silver made a call, and five minutes later, Officer Bell

pulled into the dirt drive, lights flashing blue and red over the yard. They outlined the sequence of events, and Bell relayed the information to officers who'd remained at the camp. When the ambulance arrived, Silver flat-out refused to go to the hospital. The displeased paramedic cleaned his wounds and applied bandages to his cheek and forearm.

Bell took Silver's car keys back to camp, and he returned with the Corvette. Officer Weiland followed in a squad car. They both advised them to go home.

"It will take some time to search all the buildings and surrounding woods," Weiland said.

Lindsey sensed Silver wasn't thrilled about being excluded. "I can wait here or inside one of the squad cars if you want to join the others," she suggested.

His vivid gaze swept over her and, like so many times before, she wondered what he thought of her. Not as an assistant—he'd often praised her work-related accomplishments—but as a woman. He was probably underwhelmed, considering she wasn't like the leggy model types who drooled over him.

What does it matter? We're as different as hot chocolate and apple cider. Each has its own unique appeal, but they're incompatible.

"We've had enough excitement for one night." His perfectly shaped lips pressed into a thin line. He opened her car door and walked around to his side.

Lindsey settled into the butter-soft seat. She couldn't stop fidgeting as they left the farm and traveled through unlit mountain roads. Her fingers twisted in the fuzzy collar strands of her old jacket. She studied the passing scenery, half expecting her enemy to leap from the trees and ambush them. Silver was quiet, too. No doubt wondering how he'd gotten caught up in her problem.

"If you didn't have me to worry about, what would you be doing right now?" she asked.

"I'd go to Norman's house and try to determine his whereabouts the past hour. Did he actually leave Camp Smoky or did he double back and launch an attack?"

She didn't share Silver's suspicions about the bridge repairman, but she respected his process. "Let's go then."

"I have you to worry about." The dashboard lights created hollows where his eyes were and highlighted the square bandage on his cheek.

"Drop me off at the stables then."

He didn't answer, and she caught him frowning at his rearview mirror.

"What is it?"

"Vehicle behind us, coming up fast."

They entered a section of compact curves, and headlights bore down on them. Silver pressed the gas pedal, and Lindsey's fingers dug into the door handle.

"This is a run-of-the-mill speeder, right?" She peeked at the side mirror and got an eyeful of glare. "It's Saturday. Maybe he's running late for a date."

A muscle in Silver's jaw twitched. His lips were compressed, his eyes on the strip of meandering pavement ahead. A thin guardrail followed the road on her side, protecting drivers from the deep, wooded ditch. Steep terrain bordered the oncoming lane. Not a good place to break the speed limit.

A solid thud shuddered through the Corvette, and Lindsey was thrust forward. She braced her hand against the dash. Had Silver been right about Norman?

Silver managed to keep the car between the white and yellow lines, but just barely. Another jolt, harder this time, sent the tail end swerving into the oncoming lane and the front end barreling toward the guardrail. The tires squealed in protest.

"Hang on!"

He wrestled with the steering wheel. Lindsey held her breath, begging God to intervene.

Silver managed to right the car, but the bumper skimmed the rail, metal grinding against fiberglass. They raced into the next curve. The truck's engine roared in response. It struck on Lindsey's side, near the rear wheel, spinning the car one-hundred-eighty-degrees sideways.

Her seat belt dug into her chest as Silver slammed on the brakes. The truck bore down on her, the massive grill as large as her window.

"Lindsey!"

There was a sickening crunch as the truck rammed into her door, propelling the Corvette sideways toward the rail. The window popped outward like a burst balloon. Diesel fumes choked her.

The sports car was headed for the guardrail, and there was nothing they could do to stop it. The impact jarred every bone in her body. For a split second, there was stillness. Then the truck's engine revved and the tires spun, and Lindsey's door started to cave in.

She was going to be crushed into oblivion, and Silver would pay the ultimate price for protecting her.

NINE

"Unbuckle," Silver yelled, reaching for her seat belt and pressing his window button at the same time.

No way was he letting her die. *God, please, I haven't asked You for much.*

Lindsey fumbled with the release. The instant she was free, he anchored his arm around her shoulders and gave a big tug.

"Climb onto the console! You'll exit out my window."

She struggled to get out of the seat as her side of the car began to fold in on itself.

"Hurry, Lindsey," he implored.

"The drop-off," she gasped, flopping half on the console and half on his lap. "How steep?"

"Don't know." He met her fright-filled gaze. "All I care about is getting you out of this car."

Her fingers dug into his shoulders. "I'm not leaving you behind."

Silver wasn't sure he *could* get out. His height and leg length weren't ideal for the sports car in the first place. The driver's seat was at the maximum distance from the wheel.

"You'd better not," he said, flashing a smile.

Her eyes narrowed behind her glasses, and she tilted her head. "Why—"

The door buckled inward, and plastic pieces spewed over the crumpled seat. Sweat popped out on his forehead. He hadn't thought he was claustrophobic.

"Lindsey."

Twin beams of light flashed over them from farther down the mountain. She reluctantly shimmied out the window and perched on the rail.

"Silver..." She reached for him, her hand outstretched.

His gaze hungrily soaked in her pretty features, wishing there was time to clear the air. If he didn't make it, he didn't want her dealing with a mountain of guilt.

"Climb down off the rail. If you fall, keep your elbows and knees bent and your chin tucked into your chest. Keep rolling. Don't stiffen up." Silver tried to maneuver his body out of the seat, but he was wedged in. "Go, Lindsey. Go now."

The truck's forward momentum continued, and the car's passenger side started to lift off the road. Lindsey's eyes went round with horror. She seized his collar in a death grip, as if she could extract him with a single hand.

Tires skidded to a stop, and the lights they'd noticed moments ago shone on the mangled Corvette. Car doors slammed. Shouts bounced off the hillsides.

The truck reversed so fast that Silver's car juddered to the asphalt. The stench of burning rubber filled his nostrils, and darkness blanketed the interior. Because of the angle, he couldn't see the fleeing vehicle, couldn't make out taillights or plate numbers or any other details that would help them find this guy.

Lindsey called to the bystanders. Silver watched through the cracked windshield as two young men helped her off the rail. He breathed a little easier seeing her feet on solid ground again. The pair tried to shift the rear end of the car away from the rail. It didn't budge.

A bone-chilling dread worked through him. He was trapped. Helpless. Vulnerable.

He'd been trapped in his father's basement. Locked in that dank windowless cement box for hours, awaiting punishment. The anticipation was sometimes worse than the actual beating.

He rubbed his hands down his face and attempted to talk himself off the precipice. Whenever this itchy, out-of-control feeling stole over him, he battled it with physical activity. Swimming, boxing, running. Pushing himself until his muscles quivered and begged for rest, until he was certain he could hold the memories at bay.

His father's face twisted in anger flashed in his mind. Silver was sure he could smell his expensive cologne, hear the slice of the whip through the air.

He fisted his hand and slammed it into the dash. Pain shimmered up his arm.

"Silver?"

"I need a minute," he ground out, eyes closed and jaw tight.

Surprisingly, she heeded him. But then he heard the guys' murmurs, and he opened his eyes to see her climbing over the rail. Clinging to the lip of earth on the other side, she edged toward him.

His racing heart applied the brakes. "What do you think you're doing?"

When she came even with his door, she perched on the rail. "Take my hand."

"Go back over there." He leveled his most forbidding glare at her, the one he reserved for the most defiant criminals.

She jutted her chin. "No."

"When I get out of here…"

Her brows inched above her frames. "You'll what?"

He compressed his lips and let his head fall back against the headrest.

Lindsey clamped on to the door frame, reached in and found his hand. Her fingers threaded through his, and he almost asked her to remove his glove while she was at it.

"Let's go caroling this year," she said in her planning voice. "It seems like a nice tradition, but I've never taken part. I sang with my second-grade class at the mall once. That doesn't count, though. The community would enjoy being serenaded by police officers, don't you think?"

"You obviously haven't heard me sing."

"You have a pleasant speaking voice."

The tightness in his chest began to loosen. "That doesn't translate to music."

"You can hum, surely. I can picture the four of you in your uniforms, seated on your horses. Do you think Cruz would wear a Santa hat? Oh, the horses could have ribbons in their manes and tails. You could perform in the town square."

"Why do you assume I'd wear a pointy red hat but not Cruz?"

He turned his head in her direction. She was resting one arm atop the door, and her upper body dominated the opening. Her hair swung forward and tickled his cheek.

She shrugged. "I don't know Cruz as well as I know you."

She rattled off more ideas about how to infuse a fresh slant to the holiday season. By the time the firefighters, tow-truck operator and other law enforcement arrived, he was no longer on the verge of a panic attack.

Lindsey wasn't happy about being escorted far from the Corvette. Truth be told, he missed her spunky presence… and her firm grip on his hand.

When he was finally free of the wreckage, she pushed

through the throng and burrowed against his chest. He rocked back a step. Once he'd regained his footing, he closed his arms around her and received a shock. Embracing Lindsey wasn't awkward at all. He was no longer her boss and she his employee. He rested his chin atop her head and inhaled her vanilla scent. Lindsey was soft, warm and inviting. *I could get used to this.*

Silver wasn't expecting her to shove at his midsection and glare up at him like an irate bobcat.

"Don't ever do that again."

"Do what?"

"Give up." Distress chased anger across her expressive face. "You put my safety before yours, and that's not cool."

Aware of their audience, Silver crossed his arms over his chest. "You did the same thing in the barn."

Her mouth fluttered open and closed. "That's different."

"I didn't give up. I would never do that." If that was his go-to reaction, he wouldn't have survived his father's house. He looked over the sad, mangled ruins of a car. "I've learned a valuable lesson, though. I need a bigger vehicle."

Lindsey suspected Silver was avoiding her. No wonder, considering she'd witnessed his near unraveling. Forcing a hug on the man had compounded the problem.

They'd hitched a ride home with one of the firefighters. After seeing to the dogs, snakes and birds, they had retreated to shower and change. Or so she'd thought. When she emerged from the guest bathroom, clad in her jogger pants and a long-sleeved cotton shirt, she'd heard sounds emanating from the gym. She didn't disturb him. Instead, she'd headed upstairs to the kitchen and found enough ingredients to put together a cheesy chicken casserole.

Lindsey texted with Thea. She also had a short phone conversation with her mom, careful not to mention her recent troubles. She didn't want to worry her family. There wasn't much to tell, besides the fact that a stranger harbored enough anger toward her to want her dead.

The memories of tonight's onslaught couldn't fade soon enough. Turning up the radio, she sang along with the carols. But the lighthearted songs couldn't stop her from picturing Silver in the car, unable to free himself. Her stomach knotted, and the fear was as fresh as if they were on that lonely stretch of road again.

Was this how it was for him? Did he relive every close call he'd had in his job? In those excruciating moments when he'd fought for composure, had he been having flashbacks of his childhood?

Lindsey couldn't decide whether or not she wanted to know exact details. It was painful to know he'd suffered at the hands of his own father. Worse, that she'd been his father's minion. How could Silver stand to even look at her? Much less, risk his neck for hers?

When the casserole was ready and Silver still hadn't shown his face, she went in search of him. The dogs trailed her down the stairs to the bottom level and flopped on the tile outside the gym door. She breezed inside the brightly lit space, words of confrontation on her lips. He'd been injured and nearly killed. What was he thinking? Her protest was quickly forgotten.

He was on the treadmill, lungs heaving, his tennis shoes pounding the belt. His beautiful gray hair was slicked off his forehead in damp tufts. His usually milk-white skin was flushed. He wore a sleeveless shirt, allowing her a full view of his toned, scarred arms. She drank in the sight of his bare hands. They were marble pale and crisscrossed with tiny scars. His fingers were long, like a piano player's, and the nails were short. What would he do if she made a pile of his gloves and burned them?

Heat flooded her face when she finally found his violet gaze. He'd noticed her gawking.

The machine's droning hum ceased as he punched the buttons. Lindsey got a water from the mini fridge. After he stepped off the treadmill and wiped a towel over his face, she handed the bottle to him.

"You couldn't take one day off?"

"Exercise helps burn off the frustration." The strong column of his throat worked as he guzzled the water. He reached for the sweatshirt draped over a workout bench, and she put out a hand.

"Don't do that on my account."

His lips twisted. "It doesn't disturb you?"

"Nothing about you disturbs me." Foster "Silver" Williams fascinated her.

At his hooded stare, her blush intensified.

"Are we going to talk about the panic attacks?" she said.

Another long chug. "Do we have to?"

"How often do they happen?"

"Not as frequently as in the past."

"Do you see a counselor?"

"I'm not about to spill my secrets to a total stranger." He raked his hand through his hair, leaving it in rumpled disarray. His expression turned wary. "I trust you won't pass this new information along to my parents."

"Hearthside Rentals turned out to be my dream job. I gave it up because I couldn't continue to work for you under false pretenses. I wasn't fulfilling my obligation to Gordon and Astrid anyway." He didn't look entirely convinced. "I know my word doesn't carry a lot of weight with you right now, but I wouldn't tell them what you ate for breakfast, much less that you're dealing with panic attacks."

"Not even to help your family? You still haven't told me why you owe your parents."

His continued distrust hurt more deeply than any physical wound she could sustain. Lindsey had an unfortunate habit of letting people down. *Is that my future, Lord? To be a constant disappointment to those I care about?*

She was saved from answering by an alert on his watch.

He frowned. "My grandmother just pulled into the driveway."

In all the time she'd worked for him, she had yet to meet the esteemed Hedda. "You weren't expecting her?"

"She prefers for me to come to Knoxville." He jerked open the door and held it for her. When she continued past the stairs, he said, "Where are you going?"

"To the office. Have supper with her. I'll eat once you're finished."

"You don't want to meet her?"

"Name one person in Serenity who has." He opened his mouth. "Besides Mason."

He snapped it shut.

"You're clearly protective of your relationship. I understand why."

"She's important to me," he said slowly, his fingers twisting in the towel slung around his neck. "I guess I didn't see any reason to introduce her to people who probably weren't going to be in my life long-term."

"I'm happy to give you privacy." She grazed his forearm, and he looked down at her fingers on his uneven skin.

"You're here. She's here. There's no need for you to hide in the basement."

Lindsey trailed him up the multilevel stairs. She hung back as he strode to the door and admitted his grandmother. Hedda Johansson was tall for a woman, with smooth silver hair that skimmed the collar of her powder-blue jacket. Tasteful silver jewelry adorned her ears and neck. Her eyes, the same unique hue as Silver's, were lively and intelligent. She quickly took stock of Silver's bandaged wounds.

"What happened?" She peered closely at his face.

Silver's fondness for his grandmother transformed his entire demeanor. He gently pulled her into a hug.

"We ran into a bit of trouble up at Camp Smoky," he said, easing back. "Nothing we couldn't handle."

Hedda turned to Lindsey. "Are you all right, dear?"

"I'm unharmed."

"You must be Lindsey Snow. Foster's talked so much about you that I feel I know you." Her expression was curious, open and unsmiling, but not unfriendly. "Would you be willing to tell me what happened tonight?"

Silver wagged his finger. "Gram, we agreed it's best not to burden you with the realities of my career."

"I didn't agree to any such thing."

"What brings you here late on a Saturday night?"

She indicated the plastic container in her hands. "I made *knäck*."

His brow creased. "You know I can't resist your Swedish toffee. But the curvy roads aren't safe for you to travel at night, Gram, especially on weekends when there's a higher risk of inebriated drivers."

"Last I checked, my driver's license doesn't have any restrictions, young man."

Lindsey bit her lip to hide a smile. Hedda had spunk.

Hedda's gaze bounced between them. "Since you're here together, I assume you took my advice and patched things between you?"

Silver avoided Lindsey's gaze, and she avoided Hedda's.

"I'm glad you know the truth about my daughter and her husband."

Lindsey lifted her head. Instead of derision or disdain, Hedda regarded her with compassion.

"I have many regrets." The main one was hurting Silver.

"From what he's told me, you're not the kind of person who'd take pleasure in hurting others. Owning up to our mistakes is an important part of the forgiveness process."

Silver rubbed his hands down his face. "Gram, Lindsey's had a rough day. Let's postpone this conversation until another time."

"Looks like she's not the only one," Hedda said, the creases in her brow deepening into crevices.

Lindsey gestured to the gleaming kitchen. "Why don't you join us for supper?"

"I ate earlier, but thanks for the offer."

"I could make you hot chocolate," she suggested. "Tea? Coffee?"

"Your hot chocolate has enough sugar in it to keep Gram up for days."

Hedda laughed. "Sounds irresistible. I'll take one."

Silver shook his head in exasperation, and Lindsey smiled. The chance to get to know Silver's favorite person edged out the day's troubles. Somewhere out there was an unscrupulous, determined person who'd go to great lengths to end Lindsey, no matter who got caught in the crosshairs. For now, she was safe. Her enemy wouldn't dare attempt to breach a police officer's private home. Would he?

TEN

As a rule, Silver didn't have trouble focusing during training sessions. Today was different. A killer was out there, waiting for the perfect opportunity to strike again, and he was jumping at the bit to identify him. At least they'd ruled out Norman Miller.

He and Mason had paid the repairman an early-morning visit. Norman been surprised by their questions and given them permission to search his property. They hadn't found a single weapon. He did drive a truck, but it didn't have a scratch on it. Norman's cooperation indicated he wasn't involved.

A horn blared near his ear, and he flinched. Lightning followed his nonverbal cue and skittered to the left. They were engaged in a series of desensitization drills. The horses received training every day. Once a month, their unit joined other mounted patrol units at a neighboring county's fairground facility for more in-depth conditioning. Country music swelled through the arena, and bright, searing lights pierced the generated smoke.

He and Lightning had developed their own language. Silver had to forget yesterday's assaults and the swift connection that had arisen between Gram and Lindsey. He had to stop searching for Lindsey on the perimeter. She'd stationed herself on the far bleachers to watch the proceedings, and he had to trust she wouldn't wander off.

Silver led his mount through a series of obstacles. They walked up and over a stack of pallets, through tattered, billowing flags and across a tarp. Simulated gunfire ricocheted through the airy building, followed by sirens' wails. When Mason gave the signal, they filed out of the ring and dismounted. Cruz flipped on the lights. Raven killed the blaring music and smoke machine.

He searched for Lindsey in the bleachers.

"She's over there," Raven said, removing her helmet and pointing to the opposite side. Lindsey was picking her way down the steep stairs. "You okay?"

Raven and Thorn had ridden behind him, which meant she'd likely seen his hiccups. "A little distracted, that's all."

Her eyes filled with concern, but she didn't reprimand him. They both knew that in their line of work, a little distraction was enough to get someone killed.

Lindsey reached them as they were about to exit into the parking lot where the trailers were parked. She was a billboard for Christmas in her oversize red sweater, red-and-white-striped leggings and candy-cane earrings. He had acknowledged long ago that she was pretty...in a girl-next-door sort of way. Lately, he'd begun to notice little things about her, things that pleased him. Take her eyes, for instance. They were large, fringed with the lush lashes and the shade of gingerbread.

"That was amazing," she gushed, rubbing Lightning's nose affectionately. "These horses are rock stars."

"I couldn't imagine a better partner than this guy," Silver agreed, distracted by her smile.

"Why did you leave patrol for mounted police? Did you have prior experience with horses?"

"I was ready for a new challenge." He decided to be

forthcoming. "I'd also heard horses were helpful for trauma victims."

"Equine therapy. I'm familiar with it."

"I may not have participated in an actual program, but the bond I've developed with Lightning is unlike any I've had with a person."

Her smile had a wistful quality.

Other officers began to trickle outside. They exited the stuffy interior into the feeble sunshine. The chilly air felt good against his heated skin. The parking lot was abuzz with activity. His unit was clustered in the corner near another building, and he and Lindsey joined them.

They were already in the process of untacking their horses and providing water. Cruz shot him a pointed look over Renegade's back.

"Mason mentioned that you and Lindsey ran into trouble last night."

Raven was hefting Thorn's saddle off. Her head whipped toward Silver, her gaze incredulous. "What kind of trouble? Why weren't we told about this?"

"The three of you would've descended on my house, and both Lindsey and I needed to decompress."

He relayed the bare-bones account, and then Lindsey jumped in with the gory details. Raven's eyes grew round. Cruz looked as if he could spit nails.

"What are we going to do to stop this guy?" he demanded, one hand framing his hip.

"We need a plan of action," Mason said. "We've ruled out Norman Miller. Dale Shaw is still a possible player. We need to locate him ASAP."

Silver removed Lightning's saddle and pad, then switched out the bridle for a halter. "The attacks have happened at or near Camp Smoky. We could install security cameras and set a trap."

"We make it seem like Lindsey is there alone," Raven mused. "When in reality, we'll be waiting to pounce."

Cruz rubbed his hands together. "I like it."

Silver looked at Lindsey. "You have the final say. If you're not comfortable with the plan, we'll think of a different one."

She lifted her chin. "I'll do whatever it takes to end this."

His admiration for her outshone the lingering hurt. She was clearly apprehensive, as she should be. But she was proving to him again and again that she was more than just capable and efficient. Beneath the flair, she was a woman of strength and substance—which was why he couldn't reconcile her decision to do his parents' bidding with what he knew about her.

After walking the horses to let them cool off, they loaded them into the trailers and drove the forty-five-minute return trip to Serenity.

In the feed room, Silver gathered the buckets labeled with each horse's name and asked Lindsey to measure out the sweet feed. While he was retrieving various supplements from the overhead cabinets, she received a call.

"It's my brother," she said, frowning. She angled toward the open door. "Trent? What's wrong?"

Silver measured out the supplements into the appropriate buckets. Her side of the brief conversation was stilted and disjointed. She was clearly unhappy.

"Everything okay?" he asked when she'd finished.

"I'm not sure. Trent wanted to know if I'd spoken to Eve lately. No one has heard from her in a while, and my parents are worried."

He leaned against the counter. "Do you know where she is?"

"I heard from her months ago. She called to gloat about a new boyfriend."

He sensed she was dealing with an old, festering wound. "You two aren't close?"

"Unfortunately, no. Not by my choice, either."

"I thought twins shared a special bond." She looked sad and conflicted. He squeezed her shoulder. "We don't have to discuss it."

"You deserve to know." Color climbed up her neck, and her face got splotchy. "My sister is part of the reason why I exchanged information about you for money. Eve and I used to be inseparable. I was the outgoing, headstrong twin. Eve was cautious and sensible. She was easy to sway, however, and many times I talked her into doing what I wanted. Shortly after our tenth birthday, Trent was tasked with watching us while Mom and Dad took our brothers shoe shopping. We weren't allowed to play outside when they were gone, and I got bored. I devised a game in which we used our living room as a trampoline park. We'd climb over the stair landing railing, jump over the back of the couch, leap over the coffee table and land in front of the television."

"Where was Trent?"

"In the backyard, flirting with his crush Wendy. She lived next door." Her forehead furrowed. "Eve was reluctant to join in, but she eventually caved to my wheedling. Everything was fine the first five laps. She was even having fun by that point. On the sixth go-around, she slipped and crashed into the glass coffee table." She rubbed the heel of her palm against her chest. "There was blood everywhere. She had deep lacerations on her hands, face and neck. It's a miracle she lived."

He grasped her shoulder again, but it didn't seem like enough. He could imagine her terror, as a ten-year-old, reacting to her sister's horrific injuries.

"I screamed for Trent until I was hoarse. Eve was

screaming, too." She shuddered. "I'll never forget the wild agony in her eyes."

"Did you and your brother stay at the house?"

"Wendy's mom came over and waited with us until a police officer dropped my brothers off later that night. My parents had gone straight to the hospital and remained there until the following day, when it was clear she would recover." Her eyes were dull. "Eve did eventually return home, but she wasn't the sister and confidante I'd known all my life. You see, she was left with disfiguring scars on her face and neck. Numerous surgeries couldn't erase the damage."

Silver couldn't hide his shock. Lindsey's own sister lived with scars? That explained her ready acceptance of his marred flesh.

"I can see you share Eve's opinion," she muttered. "And why not? I'm responsible for the tragedy. I'm to blame for our fractured family, for Eve's ongoing turmoil, Trent's remoteness, and my parents' worry and disappointment."

Her self-recrimination was unsettling, at odds with her can-do, fun-loving spirit. "Lindsey, you were *ten*."

"The game was my idea. I was fully aware that my parents wouldn't approve."

"Your brother was supposed to be watching you."

She rejected his attempt to defend her. "It's my fault that Eve's life is messed up. She couldn't handle her altered appearance. She became sullen and belligerent. My parents have almost gone bankrupt trying to help her, paying for counselors and equine therapy and sleepaway camps."

This was why she was familiar with equine therapy. Why she'd praised him for how he'd handled his own situation. Her sister hadn't managed so well.

"When my parents offered you the extra money, you saw a way to repay yours."

She looked miserable. "It wouldn't recoup the entire amount, of course. I gave them the bonus money and my regular pay from Williams Industrial."

Silver had jumped to the wrong conclusion. He'd assumed she'd succumbed to greed. "Do your parents blame you?"

"Not at all. They didn't want to accept the money, but they couldn't really refuse."

"Trent?"

"He blames himself. That's why he's all but cut off contact with us. He got engaged last year, and he didn't tell us. My mom heard it from a friend, who'd seen the announcement on social media."

No doubt she claimed that burden as hers to bear, as well.

"My other brothers, Thomas and Xander, are thankfully unfazed by the drama. They haven't cut us out of their lives. Eve's another story. She left Nashville shortly after graduation. For years, we had very little communication from her. We had no idea where or how she was. It tortured my parents, my mom, especially. Then she showed up at my college graduation unannounced." Her lips pursed. "She likes to cause scenes."

A part of him couldn't help but relate to Eve. "Maybe that's her way of coping."

"You didn't let your circumstances keep you from your dreams. You don't wallow in self-pity or try to spread your misery to others." She shrugged. "But who's to say I wouldn't have followed exactly the same path if I'd been in her shoes."

Silver couldn't imagine an angry, defiant Lindsey Snow. It was like picturing Christmas without twinkly lights, gingerbread men or cheerfully wrapped presents.

"All I'm saying is that you can't possibly understand what she's going through."

"I don't deny that. I wish she wouldn't shut me out. I'd like to be close again. Or to at least be included in her life. At this point, I'm beginning to think any chance of reconciliation is out of reach."

Mason poked his head in the door. "Just got a text from York. He's headed to the station to question Dale Shaw and asked if you want to be there. Shaw was picked up at Riley's Gas and Go outside town."

"I'm in." He looked at Lindsey. "You should stay here."

She accepted his pronouncement without argument, probably because she was still mulling over their conversation.

Mason entered the room and waved him out. "We'll finish this up."

Silver paused in the doorway. Lindsey stood at the counter, her head bowed and her hair cupping her cheek. He couldn't see her expression, but her slumped shoulders shouted dejection. He was gripped with the need to offer a kind word and a hug.

"Maybe I'll let York grill Shaw without me."

Mason shot him an incredulous look. "Are you serious?"

"You could go in my place."

"York didn't ask me."

Lindsey finally lifted her head. "You should go."

Understanding dawned in Mason's eyes. "Go. I've got this."

Silver left them in the tack room. *God, I don't want Lindsey to get hurt. How am I supposed to protect her and keep my emotional distance?*

Through the years, his relationship with the Lord had grown in fits and starts. He couldn't seem to overcome his past. But he needed His protection, now more than ever. His strength and wisdom, too.

Please get Lindsey through this unscathed. Help us pin-point the perpetrator. And help me to guard my heart.

He might be able to forgive Lindsey, but he would never give her the power to hurt him again.

Dale Shaw was as cool as a cucumber, despite having been plucked off the highway and summarily brought to the police station. The sandy-haired man reeked of stale alcohol and sweat. Obscene tattoos were visible above his shirt collar, and his hands were inked, as well. Across the table from Silver and Detective York, he lounged in the thin plastic chair as if he was in the comfort of his own living room. This interrogation was going nowhere fast.

"Do you deny you threatened to harm Lindsey Snow?" York said.

His smirk remained fixed, but there was no denying the ire flaring in his hooded gaze. "Don't recognize the name," he drawled. "Who is she again?"

Silver slid the file across the table and tapped the paper. "You were angry about losing your steady income, and you figured you'd get your revenge. Tell me, Shaw, how handy are you with a bow and arrow?"

"Never shot one."

"Someone shot at Lindsey and me last night," Silver said. "When that didn't work, he tried to turn my car into a pancake. Your property is close enough for you to access Camp Smoky without detection."

"What did you do, Shaw?" York rested his forearms on the table and leaned in. "Did you borrow a buddy's truck? Or maybe you stole one and then conveniently ditched it. You're aware how judges tend to view attacks on law enforcement. Add this to your existing charges, and well…"

Dale's upper lip curled. "You can't pin this on me. My hands are clean." Arrogance stamped his features. "But if my path ever does cross Lindsey Snow's, I'll make her regret ever stepping foot inside Serenity." He kept talking, detailing what he'd do to her.

Silver shot out of his chair and lunged across the table. His hands would've closed around Dale's throat if York hadn't seized his collar and yanked, cutting off his air supply.

"He's not worth it, Williams."

Officer Weiland busted into the room and, shooting Silver a commiserating glance, removed Shaw.

Fury funneled through his veins. He shoved out of his chair and kicked the table leg.

"I don't like him for this," York said calmly. In other words, he wasn't convinced Shaw was involved.

Silver stalked to the two-way glass. "You heard the way he talked about her."

"He's been playing this game most of his adult life. He knows how to get under your skin." He snapped up the folder and tapped it against his open palm. "If this is too personal, Williams—"

"It's not."

The older, more experienced officer considered him for a long, tense moment. "I'll keep digging and let you know what else I come up with." Slapping him on the back, York said dryly, "Try not to get yourself killed before we solve this."

They were out of leads. Dale Shaw was free to come and go as he pleased. His rap sheet didn't include anything close to murder. But he was furious with Lindsey. Silver worried that, given the opportunity, the guy could make good on his threats.

It was up to him to make sure he didn't get the chance.

ELEVEN

"I'm glad Mason brought you to see me." Thea was co-cooned in a jewel-colored blanket and tucked in a plush armchair, a bowl of potato soup in her hands. There was color in her cheeks, and her eyes were clear.

"I wasn't about to pass up the chance." From her spot on the couch, Lindsey could see the sergeant in the formal dining room. He had his phone pressed to his ear. Judging from his pleasant tone and generous use of sweetheart, she guessed he was talking to Tessa.

Before Silver had left the stables, silent communication had passed between the men. They were close friends who worked together on an almost daily basis, so it made sense they'd developed a nonverbal shorthand. Lindsey could only guess at the message, but she was pretty sure Silver wanted Mason to distract her—both from her current predicament and her family issues.

She was relieved that everything was out in the open. There were no more secrets between them.

"I'm sorry I wasn't able to come before now. I wanted to be with you. I wanted to ride in the ambulance, but I had to stay and tell the police what I knew." Lindsey bit her lip, reliving those terrifying moments. Her eyes smarted. "I'm glad you're home and recuperating."

"For the last time, stop apologizing," Thea admonished, a half smile softening the words. "And no more gifts, okay?"

Poinsettias and red roses were scattered throughout the room, along with balloons and a giant stuffed bear.

"It's too late to stop the shipment of gourmet cookies. They'll be delivered tomorrow. As for the truffles, I haven't ordered them yet."

"I wouldn't dream of turning down cookies or truffles." Concern invaded her eyes. "Do you think this Shaw guy is responsible?"

"I don't know." She hoped he was guilty, for everyone's sakes.

"I'm glad you have Silver to keep you safe."

"Hopefully he can quit his bodyguard duties today. Although, I'm not sure what happens to us once this is resolved. He basically told me to leave town."

"Spoken out of anger. The man is smitten with you. He just doesn't know it yet."

Thea was a romantic. Lindsey lived in reality. "Bewildered is more like it."

"Same thing." Thea took another bite of soup, then set the bowl on the side table between them. "He'll see the truth eventually—mark my words."

Lindsey wouldn't let herself envision a life with Silver. It was tantamount to emotional torture.

Mason ended his call and gestured to the front windows. "Silver's here."

When he walked into the house, Lindsey couldn't decipher his expression. She could barely see his face anyway, thanks to the giant bouquet in his hands. He carried it into the living room.

"How are you, Thea?"

She let her head fall back against the cushion and smiled up at him. "I'm getting stronger every day. Are those for me?"

"I should've known Lindsey would have this part covered," he said lightly, his smile encompassing them both.

"Thanks for everything you did to help me."

"I'm glad I was there at the right time." He placed the bouquet on the upright piano and straightened, his brilliant gaze on Lindsey. Mason lounged against the doorjamb.

"Is it over?" Lindsey asked.

"York cut him loose. He doesn't believe Shaw is guilty."

"What do you think?"

"The man didn't display any of the usual markers. Nothing suggested he was lying."

Mason rubbed his hand over his short brown hair. "York's got an uncanny ability to sniff out the truth. If he doesn't think Shaw's involved, he most likely isn't."

Silver propped his hands on his hips. "We're going to continue to monitor his movements."

Her insides churned. "What happens now?"

"We construct a web and lure him in."

He was referring to their plan to lure her would-be killer to Camp Smoky. Lindsey could barely swallow past the lump in her throat. They thought she was brave, and she wasn't going to give them a reason to think otherwise.

After returning to Silver's house, they had a casual meal of sandwiches and baked potatoes, during which they both avoided weighty topics. She left him in the living room with Wolf and Annika and went to the office. Thankfully, the temp worker hadn't changed the computer password. She logged on to her email account, printed her every correspondence with Gordon and Astrid and put them in chronological order. The process took a solid half hour, and it took another half hour to work up her nerve. Presenting Silver with this evidence felt like the right thing to do, like the final act of contrition.

Her feet were heavy on the polished treads. On the main

floor, a fire popped and hissed in the hearth and soft music filtered through the speaker. Silver lay on the couch fast asleep. Annika was curled up on the cushion near his feet. The shaggy animal lifted her head, saw that it was Lindsey and went back to sleep. Wolf, stationed on the rug near the fireplace, did the same.

Lindsey tiptoed farther into the room, entranced by his peaceful countenance. He'd changed into civilian clothes as soon as they arrived and was wearing one of those long-sleeved cotton shirts he favored—this one was navy with pencil-thin white stripes—and jeans. A decorative pillow served as a cushion for his head. His gloves lay discarded on the coffee table.

The sound of his rhythmic, steady breathing reached her. He was simply too irresistible for her peace of mind. He'd run his fingers through his hair throughout the day, to the point it had lost its styled appearance. Wayward strands fell on his forehead, softening the hard edges and planes.

She remembered the thick folder in her hands and reluctantly left it on the ottoman.

The next day, Silver parked the unit truck behind the farmer's house, climbed out and nodded a greeting to Mason, who'd driven separately. He spoke to Lindsey on the phone. "Remember what we talked about, Lindsey. Drive straight to the cabin and go inside. No detours."

"Got it."

Her voice wasn't as steady as it had been earlier at the stables. He didn't blame her. She was driving alone, straight to the scene of multiple attacks on her life.

Are we doing the right thing, God?

Silver had prayed more in the last few days than he had in the last year. This thing with Lindsey had reopened the communication lines between him and his Maker, and he was reminded how little of value he could accomplish on his own.

What if this decision puts Lindsey in inescapable danger?

Granted, the unit had constructed a solid plan that, in theory, presented minimal risk to her. That morning, Cruz had borrowed a van and gone to the camp under the guise of making repairs. Wearing slouchy clothes and a baseball hat that obscured his features, he'd pretended to inspect her cabin roof and porch awning, when he'd actually been installing security cameras.

"Raven's waiting for you."

Raven had ridden in the back of the windowless van and had slipped inside the cabin, hopefully unnoticed. She would be with Lindsey the entire night, as a last line of defense.

As soon as Cruz arrived, they would hike into camp through the same wooded area he and Lindsey had trekked through two nights before.

"I miss Hearthside," she murmured, "when the most exciting thing was a customer complaining about a malfunctioning hot tub."

He missed those days, too. He'd liked coming home, seeing her cherry-red car in the drive and anticipating what she might say or do. Lindsey had a way of injecting the element of surprise into the mundane.

"Silver?"

He'd been reaching for his Remington shotgun. At the odd note in her voice, he stopped and leaned against the truck door. "Yes?"

A long pause. "Did you read the emails?"

He blew out a breath. "Not yet."

He'd woken well after midnight to find the dogs snoozing, the fire smoldering and unexpected access into Lindsey's relationship with his parents. He'd read the first two emails and, realizing what they were, slapped the folder closed and set it aside.

"Okay."

Silver hadn't been able to sleep, driven to devour every word and at the same time repelled.

He kneaded his forehead. "Why did you go to the trouble?"

"I didn't want there to be any more secrets between us." She sighed. "I-It seemed like the right thing to do."

"I don't know if I'll read them." She didn't respond. "Lindsey?"

"I understand."

She didn't ask if he'd forgiven her. Didn't ask if he'd really meant it when he'd said she should leave Serenity. He didn't have specific answers, except that he couldn't allow her to remain in his life once the danger had passed.

Cruz's vehicle bounced over the uneven lane. Mason finished checking his ammo and holstered his weapon.

"Are you almost there?" he asked, not sure what else there was to say.

"I'm passing the gymnasium now."

Looping the gun strap over his head, he closed the door and engaged the lock. "As soon as you're inside, let me know. Cruz just got here. We'll hike in and get into place."

"Be careful, okay?"

"Stay away from the windows. Don't so much as poke your nose outside."

Raven would give her the rundown, but he felt better saying it himself. Minutes later, he heard the officer talking and knew Lindsey was safe.

Mason and Cruz were geared up, their bulletproof vests in place. Together, they crossed the open field in the gathering dusk, their night-vision goggles looped around their necks.

Lord, please protect my team and Lindsey. Bring this guy to justice before anyone else gets hurt.

TWELVE

Lindsey jolted awake, her heart thudding and skin clammy. The nightmare gradually faded as she sat upright in bed and her eyes adjusted to the shadows. Feeble light leaked around the curtains at the front-facing windows. Was it the utility pole lamp? Slipping on her glasses, she checked her phone and was surprised to discover she'd slept through the night. It was early morning, shortly after sunrise. Nothing had happened.

Their plan had failed.

The guy hadn't noticed her solitary drive to camp or had learned of law enforcement's presence. He couldn't be in all places at once. Maybe he'd gotten caught up in family or work obligations and had to set his evil agenda aside.

Climbing out of bed, she slid her feet into her sandals and pulled on her thick robe. The pallet near the door was empty.

"Raven?"

A line of light beneath the bathroom door grew into a wide triangle as Raven emerged, still dressed in her head-to-toe black. Her hair was in a neat braid.

"You're awake. Sorry if I disturbed you." Raven stowed her hairbrush in her bag.

"I can't believe I got any sleep." She'd been edgy with

nerves all evening. Raven had tried to keep her occupied with card games. "Any word from the men?"

"We didn't get him. Nothing besides the wildlife stirred last night."

Lindsey's shoulders slumped.

Raven reached out and rubbed her upper arm. "We aren't giving up, Linds."

"We can't do this every night. While I'm comfy in my bed, you four stand watch. You can't lose sleep indefinitely and still perform your regular police duties."

"A little lost sleep never hurt anyone," she said, smiling. "Get dressed, why don't you? I need my coffee."

Lindsey dragged up a responding smile and, gathering her duffel bag, trudged to the bathroom. She changed into black leggings and a plain ivory sweater, because that fit her mood today. She was brushing her teeth when an explosion rocked the cabin foundation. The toothbrush clattered to the sink as she was propelled forward, the sink lip digging into her abdomen.

A second, stronger blast knocked her to the floor as the door flew off its hinges.

Silver's comms erupted into chaos. His shock-soaked brain didn't register the terse conversation as he raced toward the damaged cabin. The porch awning had collapsed and the front wall crumbled beneath the roof. Wisps of smoke curled around the edges. From the explosion or an active fire? The rising sun winked on glass shards that had rained on the grass and gravel.

Disregarding protocol, he searched the perimeter for a way inside. Waiting for the fire department and bomb squad was out of the question.

He saw Mason approaching, his rifle at the ready. "I've got your back," he called, scanning the woods.

"EMS?"

"Cruz is in contact."

Dispatch would contact the utility company to turn off the utilities. The back of the cabin appeared to be intact. The door opened without protest, and he walked into a wall of smoke.

"Lindsey? Raven?" His high-powered flashlight revealed the destruction. No sign of the women. His gut clenched. "I'm coming in."

Please, Lord, guide me to them. Prevent further attack.

As his vision cleared, he searched for visible flames and hanging structural hazards and found none.

"Silver?"

"Lindsey!" He swung his flashlight to the right. The bathroom door wasn't on its hinges. The window had blown out, and the blinds hung by a thin string. "Where are you?"

"The shower, I think."

Cruz rushed in behind him. "EMS is ten minutes out."

Ten minutes was a lifetime if either woman had suffered serious injuries.

"Find Raven," Silver bit out. "I've got Lindsey."

Cruz gave him a thumbs-up sign.

"Are you hurt?" he asked her, seeing the door had landed near the shower.

"Nothing serious."

Fear leached out of him like a melting icicle.

He crouched down and grasped the door edges. "Lindsey, honey, I'm going to move the door."

"Okay." Her voice was small and frightened.

Silver slid it out of the room and shoved it against the opposite wall, glass bits clinking against the floorboards. The space by the sink and toilet was littered with larger shards. Daylight filtered in though a gap he hadn't noticed in the exterior wall. Thick, wide boards blocked his way to the shower.

His flashlight hit on her sock-covered feet. One sandal was missing. He couldn't see more of her, and his chest cavity felt stuffed with cotton.

"Lindsey, are you lying down or sitting up?"

"I'm on my back."

He prayed she hadn't hit her head or damaged her spine. Lightly wrapping his fingers around her toes, he squeezed. "Feel that?"

"Yes."

"Good."

He ran his light over the space, his gloved fingers following the same trail, testing and probing. A headache bloomed behind his eyes. The splintered slabs were wedged diagonally between the linen closet and the ceiling. Even if he could shift them, he didn't dare.

Cruz and Raven appeared in the opening. He had his arm around her, supporting her weight. Dust coated her body. She appeared to be in one piece. He belatedly noticed a sliver of glass lodged in her thigh.

"Your leg—"

"It's minor," she said, covering her mouth as coughs racked her. "Lindsey?"

"I'm talking with her now." He eyed Cruz. "Send the fire department guys in here ASAP."

"You got it."

They continued outside, and Silver set his flashlight on the ground.

"Do you want the good news or the bad news first?"

"I'm stuck in here, aren't I?" The wobble in her voice stabbed at his heart.

He crouched down and placed his hand on her ankle, lightly rubbing the skin above her sock. "We have to wait for the professionals. I don't want to risk digging you out and possibly bringing the beams down on our heads."

Silver glanced down. Daylight was taking hold, giving him a clearer view. There was maybe an inch between her legs and the slabs. Silver felt a burst of gratitude. A little lower, and she could've suffered crushed bones.

"The good news is I'm treating you to a full-on breakfast. Pecan waffles, your favorite, with bacon, eggs and grits."

She didn't respond the way he'd hoped. "Do you think there are more bombs? Is he watching us, waiting for the right time to detonate the rest?"

"He knows law enforcement is about to descend on this place. He's not sticking around." Silver didn't mention the other possibilities, like timers or unstable devices that failed to detonate the first time.

"You have to leave," she said suddenly, trying to shift positions.

"Stay still, Lindsey." He grasped both her ankles and prayed the structure would hold.

"Get out, Silver. Please. I'll be fine here by myself."

Her tone told a different story. He wished he could see her face. "No can do."

The fire chief, when he arrived, had other ideas. "I'm not going to argue with you, Officer Williams. We can't do our jobs if we're having to work around you."

Silver opened his mouth to protest, but Lindsey piped up. "I'll be okay. Go check on Raven."

He had the fierce need to hold her close. Maybe he was resistant to leaving more for his sake than hers.

The chief gripped his shoulder. "We're going to take good care of her."

He nodded, his throat thick, as if he'd swallowed a pine cone. "I'll be outside waiting for you, Lindsey."

He waited for a witty comeback. All he heard was what sounded like a sniffle.

Outside, he bent and propped his hands on his knees, sucking fresh air into his lungs. Mason appeared at his side. "The sheriff's department has promised to help search the area. How is she?"

"Alert. Scared." He straightened, self-directed anger choking him. "Why didn't I think of this scenario?"

Firefighters urged them to move farther out. Mason put a hand on his shoulder and guided him around to the front, still within sight of the cabin but out of the hot zone. Several ambulances were parked behind the fire engine.

"We all underestimated him," Mason said tightly, his brown eyes smoldering. "We won't do that again."

Silver removed his gloves, shoved them into his pocket and scrubbed his hands down his face. "Why is God allowing this?"

He'd entertained the same question throughout his career, mostly when innocents got hurt and lawbreakers got away.

"I don't have an answer for you. When things were crazy with Tessa and her brother, I kept coming back to the verse everyone likes to quote, Romans 8:28. *And we know that all things work together for good to them that love God, to them who are called according to* His *purpose.*" He gestured to the destruction. "In this case, I'm thinking of a different passage. *To console those who mourn in Zion, To give them beauty for ashes, The oil of joy for mourning, The garment of praise for the spirit of heaviness.*"

Silver thought about those Scriptures. His and Lindsey's connection had been obliterated by his parents' schemes and her role in them. But he still cared about her. That hadn't changed. Things were going from bad to worse, but

God could certainly restore things to rights. He had to trust in His promises, no matter what happened.

Lindsey sensed the daylight growing brighter around her, but she couldn't see much in her dark hole. The shower floor pattern was imprinting itself onto her back, and the metal drain was becoming uncomfortable.

As the firefighters discussed their options, her heart quivered like a nervous bird desperate to escape its cage. She hadn't been trapped before. It wasn't pleasant. Lindsey understood how Silver had felt, trapped in his car on that mountain road.

She could really use his reassuring touch right now. *Thank You, Lord, that I have on clean, cute socks with no holes in them.*

"You're going to hear some loud pounding," a deep voice informed her.

"Okay."

With each strike, the wooden obstruction and the floor beneath her vibrated.

I need You, Jesus. You're my best friend. This was the prayer she said when in the dentist chair. *Please, hold my hand.*

Another jarring jolt dislodged water from the shower spigot, raining ice-cold drops on her face. She squealed, and the pounding stopped.

"You all right, Lindsey?"

No, I'm not all right. I haven't been all right for weeks. Months, even.

"Um, yeah."

They started up again, and she squeezed her eyes tight and pictured Jesus holding her hand, imparting His strength to her.

"We're all set out here. You're going to hear a buzzing sound. That's the saw cutting through the barrier."

"Okay."

The machine growled to life, its roar assaulting her ears.

She opened her eyes. Her glasses had been cracked during the initial blast, but she was grateful they hadn't fallen out of reach.

She kept her eye on the saw's metal teeth. The top section didn't look sturdy. In fact, it looked as if it was about to dislodge.

Lindsey yelled out a warning, but they couldn't hear her.

It tipped toward her.

Her scream bounced off the shower walls.

THIRTEEN

The saw stopped. Gloved hands wrapped around the unstable section and kept it from smashing her face. Not the refined leather gloves she associated with Silver. These were the bulky gloves firefighters wore.

"What's going on?"

Silver had returned, and his tone indicated he was not pleased. She could picture his exact expression.

"Williams, I already told you to steer clear."

"I heard her screaming. What did you do? Lindsey, talk to me."

"I'm okay."

There were more charged words exchanged. The saw started up again, drowning them out. When the final piece of the barrier was removed, three men stared down at her. Silver wasn't among them.

Eager to see him and the bright, open sky, she started to sit up. Her rescuers insisted she remain still in case of spinal or neck damage. She had to wait for them to put on a neck collar, slide the backboard beneath her, strap her in and carry her out.

He was waiting beside the back door, and his stormy violet eyes raked over her again and again. His face was streaked with grimy lines of sweat. His hair was in disarray. He was distressed over her, and that fascinated her.

He stepped forward, stopping their progress. "Lindsey." He took her hand between his bare ones, bent and kissed her temple.

Every nerve sat up and took notice. Her skin burned where his lips touched.

His fingers tightened, and he speared the guys bearing her weight with a grumpy glare. "I'm not leaving her."

They didn't dispute his statement, and they quickly got her situated in the ambulance. Silver climbed in after her. Mason popped his head in and promised to meet up with them later. Raven had already left for the hospital, they told her. Her injuries appeared to be minor.

Silver watched every move the paramedic made as he checked her vitals.

"You're sure Raven's okay?"

"I saw her with my own eyes," he responded, "upright and walking on her own steam."

Gratitude crashed over her, and with it, a rush of emotion. She closed her eyes, but a couple of rogue tears escaped.

"Ma'am? Are you experiencing any discomfort?"

Silver's incredibly smooth hand covered hers where it lay on the gurney. "Lindsey?"

She returned the pressure, taking immense comfort from the contact. "No, no. I'm just grateful no one was seriously injured." Or killed.

This game her enemy was playing was intensifying at a terrifying rate.

"The Lord protected you both," Silver said.

She opened her eyes and was met with an intense look she couldn't quite decipher. "I'm glad you're here with me," she whispered, her cheeks heating at the paramedic's questioning look.

"I wouldn't be anywhere else."

Silver checked his phone again for a missed email or text. Lindsey noticed and balanced her fork on the plate's edge. They'd come home straight from the hospital. While she showered and changed, he'd fixed the breakfast foods he'd promised. It was going on noon, but she didn't seem interested in eating.

"Still no word?"

"Not yet." He gestured to the coffee table. "You've barely touched your food."

Seated in the middle of his sofa, she sank against the soft cushions, pulled her knees to her chest and wrapped her arms around herself. "I'm not hungry."

She looked so small and vulnerable. He couldn't resist going to her. Angling toward her on the couch, he reached over, caught a stray lock and smoothed it behind her ear.

Her startled gaze delved into his, and her lips parted.

To his surprise, he didn't want to stop at a simple caress. He couldn't think of a single thing to say because his mind was at war. Cross the line of professionalism he'd drawn between them? Take a risk on someone who'd hurt him? Risks were part of his job, not his personal life.

Lindsey decided for him. Her lashes sweeping down, she picked at a stray thread on her sleeve. "The camp repair budget will need to be reexamined. I dread telling Eugene."

Silver lowered his arm, both relieved and disappointed. "Wait until tomorrow."

"I'd let myself believe this would be over today." Her lower lip trembled. Taking in a deep, bracing breath, she pressed her fingers hard against her mouth.

"Hey." He squeezed her shoulder. "We will catch this guy."

While Cruz was manning the stables, Mason was working in conjunction with the sheriff's department to scour the area. The security feeds had revealed nothing of value. The perp had to have planted the devices in previous days, probably in the hopes Lindsey would return. He could've even wired the place to alert him of her presence.

"What about my friends? What about the unit? What about you?" Her big eyes locked onto him, pleading for reassurances he couldn't give. "What's he going to blow up next? Today was really close, Silver. What if he's successful next time?"

Silver curved his arm around her and eased her against his side. She came willingly, resting her head on his chest. Her small hand splayed on his ribs.

"Don't let your mind go down that path," he murmured, his senses working overtime to drink her in. Lindsey was in his arms, and it felt nice. Better than nice, actually.

Although midday, the tree was lit up, merry and cheerful against the drab skies visible through the windows. She'd decorated the day after Thanksgiving and, as in the previous year, roped him into helping. He'd grumbled out of principle, but she'd persevered in her mission to bring holiday cheer to his home. And he'd enjoyed himself.

"Was Christmas always your favorite holiday?" he asked.

"Always."

The smile in her voice said he'd hit on the right topic to lift her spirits. "What was it like for your family?"

"Busy. Exciting. Dreamy. Kind of like a holiday movie, but without the snow."

"Yeah, a white Christmas in Nashville occurred only twice in my memory."

"Snow or not, we made the most of it. We hosted cookie swaps, serenaded the nursing-home residents, wrapped presents at the mall for charity."

"I guess there were heaps of presents for you to open. Were you the kind to sneak peeks?"

She sat upright. "Me? Ruin the surprise? No way. The anticipation buildup to Christmas morning was part of the thrill. You forget my parents were on a tight budget, and there were five kids. My mom was really good at making us feel blessed, even though we didn't have much." Her eyes were soft and bright, her smile wistful. "Things changed after Eve's accident. It wasn't quite so holiday-card-perfect. Maybe that's why I try so hard to recapture the magic. Someday, if I have children of my own, I plan to make it special for them. And of course, make sure they remember the main point—celebrating Christ's birth."

It was no stretch to picture Lindsey with kids. She'd be a fantastic mom. Something about that image filled him with longing, which was strange.

"Were your holidays difficult?" she asked.

"The opposite of a movie. My parents had the office building decorated, but not the house. When I was younger, my nanny, Ruth, insisted on putting a tree in my room. We made paper chains each year and strung popcorn." He smiled. "She'd bring me homemade cookies. They were crescent shaped and rolled in powdered sugar, and she didn't mind that I got it all over my clothes. She'd also give me a gift, which I'd hide from my parents."

"Why?"

"They'd make me return it or donate to charity. I learned that the hard way."

Her forehead bunched. "That's terrible. Why didn't they want you to have gifts?"

"My father was determined not to spoil me. They did

give me a book each year, and they allowed me to keep Gram's package that arrived in the mail." On a whim, he stood and held out his hand. "I'd like to show you something."

Curiosity brightening her expression, she slipped her hand in his and allowed him to help her up. He led her down the stairs to the middle floor, into his bedroom and the generous closet he'd had built of cedar.

Her eyes were huge, taking everything in. Silver strode to the corner cabinet and hefted out three fabric boxes. He set them on the waist-high storage cabinet in the middle and removed the lids.

"These are from Ruth."

Lindsey assessed the items. He felt a little self-conscious. To the casual observer, these gifts weren't worth a whole lot. Some might even call it junk. But each one had brought a bit of joy into his harsh life, and he treasured them.

She lifted her hand, only to pause midair. "May I?"

"Of course."

She chose a die-cast motorcycle and held it in her palm. "Ruth must've cared a great deal about you."

"She's a special lady."

"Are you in contact with her?"

"Ruth and her family live in Nashville. I haven't seen her in several years, since before I joined the mounted unit. We talk on the phone every month or so, and she sends birthday and Christmas cards each year."

Exchanging the motorcycle for a stuffed polar bear, she ran her fingers over the threadbare white fur. "This guy looks well loved. How old were you when she came to work for your family?"

"Six." Although his initial mistrust had been significant, it hadn't taken him long to warm to her. "She was nurturing, kind and gentle. Everything my parents weren't. I once asked her to take me home with her."

Lindsey reached across the counter and covered his hand with hers. "I think God placed her in your life to help you cope."

"I never thought of it that way." He stared at the floor for a long moment. "There were others besides her. Mr. Howard, my middle-school debate teacher, saw potential in me. Whenever I wanted to quit the team, he'd encourage me to give my best effort. *If you want something bad enough*, he'd say, *you'll put your all into it*. I didn't want to disappoint him, so I did what he suggested. In high school, I had a math teacher who spent countless afternoons helping me master equations. Patience must've been her middle name, because I really struggled. In the end, I got a passing grade because of her."

Lindsey's smile was wistful as she carefully returned the polar bear to its spot. "I wish I'd known you then. I would've liked to be your friend."

"I doubt I would've been a good friend then. I had a lot of bottled-up anger inside. I was focused on my own misery and wouldn't have cared about your problems."

Two bright spots appeared on her cheeks. "That's not the case now."

Silver was intrigued by her blush. Did she know he'd become hyperaware of her every move, sigh and expression? Did she realize that being near her was quickly becoming an exercise in self-control? That he didn't know how to handle these new feelings?

What if he made the wrong move, and it blew up in his face? What if he lowered his guard and got burned again?

Showing her his prized possessions and giving her an intimate glimpse into his past probably wasn't the smartest idea. As tempting as it was to spend the remainder of the day with her, he didn't want a repeat of that cozy couch situation.

He replaced the boxes in the cabinet and ushered her to his bedroom door. "I'm going to get in some exercise."

Lindsey hesitated. Disappointment was quickly eclipsed by a fake smile. "I'll be in the office. I've got to finish wrapping the gift baskets for tomorrow's event."

Serenity held a yearly fundraiser to aid various children's charities, and it drew folks from surrounding communities. As in years prior, Hearthside Rentals had secured a spot. When Lindsey had reminded him about it, he'd given her two choices—find someone to take her place or withdraw.

"Mason's sister is still set to take your place at our booth, right?"

"Candace promised to be there. We just have to unload the baskets and free merchandise and give her a brief explanation of how we do the giveaways." She nudged her glasses up her nose. "Do you mind if I watch a movie later in the living room?"

"Make yourself at home."

"I could wait for you…"

He would like that. "Thanks, but I've got other stuff to do."

What a lame excuse. Stuff? What stuff?

But she accepted it with aplomb and went downstairs to the office. He stood there, debating whether or not to help her with the baskets, until he heard Christmas tunes. Then he closed the door.

FOURTEEN

"I don't know why I agreed to this," Silver muttered, pacing the length of the decorated table and studying the people trickling into the resort conference space. He should've arranged to drop off their things yesterday.

Lindsey readjusted the cellophane-wrapped baskets and auction slips. Each basket was themed and packed with goodies, along with a coupon for a weekend at one of their cabins.

"I'm less nervous in this crowded, public space than I was in the cabin."

Lips pursed, he checked his watch. "Candace is ten minutes late."

"She will be here. Maybe she's having trouble finding a parking space."

Lindsey stared at the sea of happy faces and wished she could stay and interact with them. Last year, she had represented Hearthside Rentals. She'd handed out chocolate bars stamped with their logo, writing pens and miniature tote bags.

When she'd reminded him Hearthside Rentals was committed to sponsor a booth in today's event, he'd wanted to withdraw. Fortunately, Candace Reed had agreed to take her place. Lindsey had convinced him to let her set up the cabin photos, banner and baskets. This was a great opportunity to advertise and help the community.

"I'm sorry I'm late!" Candace emerged from the vendor entrance, trailed by Mason, Tessa and Lily. "My car wouldn't start, and Mason had to double back and pick me up." Stowing her purse beneath the table, she pushed her fingers through her short blond hair. "What do you need me to do?"

"Thanks for doing this." Lindsey explained the basics. "If someone has a question about the cabins that you can't answer, please text me."

"Uncle Silver!" Lily raced over to him and jumped up and down. "I'm getting a pony for Christmas!"

Lifting the four-year-old into his arms, he looked at her in surprise. "You are? A real live one or a stuffed one?"

"Real. Right, Daddy?" She pushed her nut-brown curls off her face and peered at Mason, who was helping Tessa out of her coat.

He chuckled. "I don't recall agreeing to that, ladybug."

Lily blinked up at Silver. "Will you get me one, Uncle Silver? Please?"

Tessa cut off his answer. "Don't even think about it." Sidling between their table and the one belonging to the Mint Julep Boutique, Tessa hugged Lindsey. "I'm so sorry you're facing this trial," she murmured against her hair. "How can I help?"

Lindsey pulled back. "Just pray."

Tessa's hazel eyes were sympathetic. "You were such a blessing to me when I was in trouble. I'd like to be the same for you."

"Thanks, Tess. I'll let you know if I think of anything. Silver's taking good care of me."

Lindsey's gaze found him automatically, as it tended to

do. The sight of the strong, solemn gray-headed officer absorbing Lily's animated chatter made her smile.

"Mason said Silver's worried sick about you."

"He feels responsible for me. Plus, I don't have family here."

"It's more than that, I think."

"He's a cop. Protecting people is in his DNA."

"Would Weiland or Bell glue themselves to your side in an effort to keep you safe?"

Lindsey looked at Silver again and caught him staring. Lily had scampered down and was tugging Mason's hand, pointing to the kids' activity area.

His thoughts—and his feelings about her—were anyone's guess. That he had shown her his childhood treasures meant a lot. He'd avoided her for the rest of the day, though, and she couldn't help thinking he regretted the decision.

The men approached. "Tess, do you mind taking Lily to the crafts? She wants to paint a picture frame. I need to talk to Silver and Lindsey."

"Not at all."

Going on tiptoe, Tessa lifted her face for a kiss. Mason willingly obliged, his smile speaking of a deep-down joy that Lindsey could only dream about. She was glad the couple had found happiness at last. After all they'd been through, they deserved it.

"I have an update," Mason said. The three of them moved behind the row of tables and against the partition wall. "Dale Shaw has been cleared from involvement in your case, Lindsey. We can't prove he has access to the plant-based toxin. We can't link him to the truck incident and he has an airtight alibi for the time frame in which the bombs were planted."

"Where does that leave us?" Lindsey asked.

"During the search of Camp Smoky, the sheriff's department discovered an abandoned campsite."

Silver's arms dropped from their folded position. "And we're just learning of this today?"

"They didn't find any solid clues. There was a sleeping bag and an empty box of cigarettes. Looks like it's been there awhile. They're thinking it could be a random drifter, but they're conducting a fingerprint analysis." Mason shifted his stance, his gaze cutting between them and the crowd. "The crime lab is examining the remnants of the improvised explosives."

Candace appeared at Lindsey's elbow. "Sorry to interrupt. There's a man over here asking for you."

Silver's body language went from casually alert to battle mode in an instant. His hand went to his waist, where the outline of his weapon was visible beneath his shirt.

Lindsey edged to the side and, glimpsing the man in question, put a restraining hand on Silver's arm. "Relax—it's Albert Bartosz." To Mason, she said, "Albert is one of our repeat customers. He's a widower and lives north of Knoxville. He likes to bring his adult sons to Serenity several times a year for bonding time."

Candace returned to her station. Lindsey followed close behind and, stepping into the flow of visitors, greeted Albert with a smile.

"I haven't seen you at one of these fundraisers before. How did you hear about it?"

"I saw an ad online." About her father's age, Albert was short and stout, with a pleasant demeanor. He held out a white poinsettia wrapped in red cellophane. "This is for you."

"What a thoughtful gift, Albert. Thank you."

As she accepted the potted plant, she sensed Silver close beside her.

"Hello, Mr. Bartosz," he greeted in his stark, official police business voice.

Albert smoothed his thinning red hair. "Mr. Williams."

"Did you bring your sons with you today?" Silver asked.

"No, they were too busy to make the trip." Albert moved out of the way to let a mom and stroller pass. He gestured to their table. "I thought I'd check out your auction items. You know how much I enjoy staying in your cabins."

"We really appreciate the guests you've sent our way," she said.

"You care about your guests." He beamed at Lindsey. "They say customer service is dead these days, but I have to disagree. You treat us like family." He slanted her a sly look. "Speaking of family, Devon was asking about you the other day. I wouldn't mind having you for a daughter-in-law."

Silver made a garbled sound in his throat. Thrusting the poinsettia into his hands, she looped her arm through Albert's and steered him to the table.

"That's sweet of you to say, but I don't date clients."

"It's your boss, isn't it? He forbids it? I could talk to him—"

"No, no. That's not necessary." She didn't bother to inform Albert that she was no longer with the company. Silver hadn't wanted to linger and launching into an explanation with this particular customer would take some time. "What do you think of our selection? You might like this New Year's Eve package. Or the spring getaway."

As soon as he decided which one to bid on, Silver intervened.

"Mr. Bartosz, Lindsey and I have to go. Enjoy your visit."

Before he could respond, Candace distracted him, waving the basket of free chocolate beneath his nose.

Silver's hand settled on her lower back as they navigated the crowd. Mason had already joined Tessa and Lily at craft central.

"You're going to dig into his life, aren't you?"

He shouldered open the vendor door. "Yep."

"He's a loyal customer," she countered, walking past him.

"Loyal to the service we provide or to you?"

She sighed, unable to picture Albert as an evil mastermind. The door clanged shut, muffling the music and conversation. The carpeted hallway around the resort's perimeter was deserted.

"I don't like being suspicious of every person I come into contact with."

"Your life is at stake, Lindsey. I'm going to investigate every potential threat."

She stopped walking. "I'm not used to this side of you, you know."

As her boss, he'd been patient and willing to entertain her ideas. Around his friends, he was easygoing and quick with witty comments. Before that first arrow struck Thea, he would've engaged someone like Albert Bartosz in friendly conversation.

He turned back, pale brows pinched and his jaw tight. "Having someone I care about with a target on her back is new to me."

Her stomach dipped. "You care about me?"

His eyes shifted between turbulent blue and wounded purple. He pinched his lips together, as if determined not to let any more ill-timed admissions escape.

The door whooshed open, and a pair of resort employees came through pushing garbage bins on wheels. Silver focused on the young men, and there went her chance of getting an explanation.

Lindsey smothered a groan of frustration. Then her phone rang, and she saw the caller's name.

"Who is it?" Silver asked.

"Camp Smoky's owner, Eugene Butler. He must've heard about the cabin."

Silver watched the emotions play over Lindsey's face. He gathered from her side of the conversation that a concerned neighbor had alerted the property owner. She paced from one side of the hall to the other, worrying her lower lip and toying with her earring. The light from the suspended fixtures glinted off her glasses.

His thoughts returned to his slipup. Sure, he cared about her, but nothing had changed.

God, I'm not used to coming to You for advice. I make decisions and deal with the ramifications. But I'm starting to see that's not how this relationship is supposed to work. Help me change. At the moment, I need self-control. I have to resist the growing pull Lindsey has over me. She looks at me like I'm the most important person on the planet, and that makes me want to forget she ever knew my parents.

She ended the call and slipped the phone in her coat pocket. "He's upset that I didn't call him and that Raven and I were inside when it happened."

"Understandable. Since it's his property, he could potentially be held liable for injuries."

"I reassured him that we're both fine. He informed me that his adult children want him to sell Camp Smoky and split the proceeds."

"Will he?"

"He doesn't want to. He and his late wife built and operated the camp together."

"He's holding on to it for her memory's sake."

"Eugene also knows how much happiness it brings to

visitors. There's the tax revenue it generates for the county. Local businesses also benefit."

"What are his expectations of you in the meantime?"

"Continue with the repairs I've already scheduled. He asked that I stay away from the property as much as possible. That means I won't be able to oversee the day-to-day progress. He could get swindled."

"I'm surprised he didn't fire you." Her spine stiffened, and he held up a hand. "Although you're not at fault for the damage, it would be in his best interests to hire someone else."

The starch went out of her posture. "Someone who isn't marked for death, you mean."

"Please don't use that phrase again, Lindsey." A text came through, and he skimmed it. "Weiland responded to a call about an abandoned truck that's been wrecked. It's been towed to the police station. Want to swing by before we go to the stables?"

Lost in thought, she absently agreed. The resort was located about a mile from the station. Once there, they met Weiland in the closed-off lot behind the building. Lindsey located his crushed Corvette at the same time as him, and her face dimmed. He reached out and gave her hand a gentle squeeze.

The patrol officer strode to the only truck in the lot, a heavy-duty work pickup with plenty of engine power to crush his compact sports car. "You can see the damage to the front bumper and grill. The right headlight is crushed."

Silver crouched down for a better look. "Black paint, the same color as my car."

Memories of that isolated mountain road taunted him, and the sensation of being trapped invaded his body. He stood, breathing the crisp air in through his nostrils and out through his mouth. Lindsey took hold of his hand again.

He gazed down into her velvety brown eyes, recalling how brave she'd been that night, how determined she'd been not to leave him. He didn't know how long his distraction lasted. Long enough for Weiland to clear his throat and shoot him a shrewd look.

"We're going to transport this to the sheriff's crime scene unit garage later today," he said.

"This is the break we've needed." Silver's gaze returned to the sports car he'd owned for less than two years. It looked like a squashed bug. "Surely our guy left something of his behind."

Lindsey toyed with her jacket zipper. "That would mean a return to our normal lives."

Silver wanted nothing more than this guy to be locked away for good and Lindsey to be safe. But what did "returning to normal" mean for them? Since learning of her connection to his parents, he hadn't asked her to come back to Hearthside Rentals. Initially, he hadn't even wanted her to stay in Serenity.

What did he want now? What did she want?

FIFTEEN

As Silver drove up his driveway, Lindsey admired the miniature white lights on the hedges and their reflection on the glass. Spotlights lit up the exterior and a portion of the yard close to the house. The woods beyond the yard, however, presented an impenetrable wall of black.

While she considered his home a safe haven, she was becoming suspicious of every place and unknown face. Her outlook, her day-to-day activities, were being shaped by a stranger. The only bright spots in her life were the friends who'd stepped up to help her in her time of need.

As she studied Silver's profile, a lump lodged in her throat. Silver Williams had once been a mysterious figure, a person she'd heard and wondered about but never dreamed she'd meet. Now he was her most devoted protector. And he cared about her.

He'd actually said the words. A little thrill, like a rare, beautiful butterfly, winged through her. The thrill dissipated. He'd regretted the admission. And why wouldn't he? She didn't deserve his trust or kindness. She definitely didn't deserve his friendship or anything more. She'd let her twin sister down, her family down and now him.

He put the borrowed unit truck in Park and caught her staring. "What's on your mind?"

She released her seat belt and clasped her purse to her middle. "Did I ever tell you I saw you at Williams Industrial?"

"No, you didn't. When?"

"During my third year of college. I'd recently started my internship, and I was making massive amounts of copies one morning when I overheard some employees saying you were nearby. I was curious, so I went out into the hallway and saw you waiting for the elevator." She smiled, remembering she'd been a tad awestruck by him. "Your hair was dark brown then, but liberally streaked with gray."

"Ah, the salt-and-pepper stage. I was tempted to go ahead and dye it, but I never got around to it." His mouth quirked. "I can't imagine why I would've been there. I rarely visited the office."

"Your presence caused quite the stir." He'd captured her imagination. She'd thought of him off and on over the next few years, wondering about his life. "I thought you must have the most glamorous lifestyle."

"That's what my parents wanted people to think."

"People in the office referred to you as Foster. Your parents and Hedda call you that, too. When did you get your nickname?"

A soft laugh escaped. "At the academy, the instructors gave just about everyone nicknames. Mine was an obvious choice. My hair was completely gray by then."

"You didn't mind?"

"I decided I liked being called by a name other than the one my parents picked out." Tapping his window, he said, "We'd better let the dogs out. It's been hours."

By the time Lindsey emerged from the truck, Silver had disarmed the alarm and released Wolf and Annika. The twin beasts streaked down the driveway and into the grass. She and Silver descended the concrete steps tucked between the pavement and the house. As soon as the dogs finished their business, they began to chase each other in an effort to bleed off excess energy.

She was going to miss spending time with him. As soon as this case was solved, he'd cut her out of his life. She'd have to mourn what she'd lost all over again.

Was it right to stay in Serenity against his wishes? Wasn't that a selfish act?

She'd insisted on having things her way one too many times with Eve, and her sister's life had been ruined.

His phone rang. "It's Gram."

He answered the call and drifted closer to the drive. In order to give him privacy, Lindsey began to play with the dogs. Wolf and Annika were thrilled to have her undivided attention. She found one of their balls and began a game of fetch. Before long, Annika abandoned the game and raced into the woods beyond the outdoor pool.

Lindsey darted in after her, calling her name. Pine needles snagged her hair. She ducked out of the way, only to get whacked in the face with a pine cone. The trees grew close together here, and the shadows were the consistency of molasses. A sense of foreboding crawled over her.

"Annika!" She heard the patter of paws on the uneven terrain, but she couldn't see the dog. "Want a treat?"

The promise of dog treats usually did the trick. She gasped as a dark shape bundled past her, its hulky body brushing her legs.

"Wolf! Come back!"

She advanced a couple of steps, arms held aloft to maintain her balance. The slanted ground was spongy, with a carpet of decaying leaves and pine needles. Something rustled farther up the hillside, and she flinched.

Her attacker was familiar with Camp Smoky. Had his failures to kill her there made him alter his plans?

"Annika? Wolf?"

A twig snapped. Her pulse tripped over itself. That sounded like a heavy boot cracking thin wood.

Overactive imagination or not, she couldn't go after Silver's dogs alone. Lindsey turned to retreat. The house lights were vaguely visible through the intertwining branches.

"Stop her."

The command splintered the silence, and she sensed someone directly behind her as something snaked around her throat and squeezed.

She clawed at the thick leather strap, unable to draw air, unable to scream.

Incessant barking interrupted his conversation, and he turned to find his yard empty. "Gram, I gotta go."

Shoving the phone in his pocket, Silver jogged toward the woods and removed his Glock from his holster.

Lindsey and the dogs had been here minutes ago. At the tree line, he slowed and ducked into the woods, taking a moment to get his bearings. Nothing around him moved. His eyes could barely penetrate the shadows, but he wasn't going to turn on his flashlight and perhaps become a target. He followed his dogs' barking, straight ahead and slightly downhill.

The farther he trekked without crossing paths with Lindsey or hearing her voice, the more convinced he became that she was in trouble.

Voices raised in argument shattered the silence, and his body tensed. These were trespassers on his property, and he was pretty sure their presence wasn't a coincidence. Had they been dealing with two perps all along? Or had their guy gotten impatient and enlisted help?

"You should've shot the dogs."

"I'm not shooting a dog."

The second voice vibrated with annoyance, but that's not what startled Silver. It belonged to a woman.

"The cop's going to come looking for her," the man retorted, his words strained. "How much farther to the car?"

Silver couldn't make out the muffled response. Lindsey's silence felt like a band around his chest. Possible reasons for it pounded his brain. He couldn't let the terror building inside derail his instincts.

He moved as swiftly and silently as he could, trying to avoid dislodging the soft earth. He stayed slightly above their position. They weren't traveling at the same rate of speed, and he quickly closed in on them. There was a break in the trees, and he was finally able to make out their shapes—one tall and broad-shouldered, the other of average height. The man was walking in an ungainly pattern, thanks to the extra weight he was shouldering.

Lindsey.

Sweat popped out on Silver's forehead. His options were limited. He couldn't use his weapon against them, not with Lindsey in the line of fire. He decided on the element of surprise.

Silver let loose an ear-piercing whistle, praying his dogs would respond. The woman spun and fired. He dove behind a tree.

Wolf and Annika burst into the small clearing and created the diversion he needed.

The woman backed away from the growling dogs and melted into the shadows. Wolf latched onto the man's ankle, and Lindsey went down. A moan escaped at impact—the most beautiful sound to greet his ears in a long while. Although he didn't know the extent of her injuries, she was alive.

Silver advanced toward them, his gun outstretched. The man noticed and, dislodging Wolf with a violent shake, sprinted down the hillside. If his chief concern hadn't been to get Lindsey to safety, he would've pursued him. Silver commanded the dogs to stay with him.

He scooped her up and carried her through the dark woods. Once in the safety of his yard, he laid her on the grass.

"Lindsey, honey, can you hear me?"

He ran his hands along her sides, searching for obvious fractures. He didn't see any bullet or knife wounds.

Her forehead bunched, and she groaned.

"I'm taking you to the hospital."

"No, not again." Her lashes fluttered, and she opened her eyes. "My throat hurts, and I have a killer headache, but I'm okay."

"You're sure?"

She'd lost her glasses somewhere, and her eyes were huge and dark. "Positive."

He helped her sit up. "Can you see without your glasses?"

"Not far away, but I can manage. I won't be able to read without them."

"We'll call first thing in the morning and order a new pair." He glanced over at the woods. "Let's get you inside. Can you walk?"

She nodded, but she wobbled once she was on her feet. Silver scooped her into his arms again, and she gasped. "A warning might've been nice," she wheezed, her icy fingers pressing into the back of his neck.

"Sorry." Wolf and Annika trailed at his heels as he carried her up the stairs and through the front door. "Couch okay?"

"Yes, please."

As soon as he had her settled, he called Dispatch and gave them the perps' last known location.

"Is there more than one person after me?" Lindsey was flanked on both sides by his dogs, who were licking her hands.

Silver lured them off the couch with treats. He returned with a bottled water for her.

He took the spot beside her and removed his gloves. "A man and a woman," he confirmed. "Do you remember anything?"

"I went after Annika. I didn't go far, even when Wolf joined her. I was about to come and get you when someone attacked me from behind." Letting the unopened bottle fall onto its side, she touched her throat and winced.

Silver scooted closer and nudged her hand aside. He trailed his fingertips along the edge of the linear red marks and felt his anger spark into a roaring flame. Her eyes were locked onto him. She shivered.

He closed his eyes and concentrated on his breathing, tamping down the thirst for vengeance. Silver sometimes felt as if he was walking a tightrope between his desire to see evil punished and his pledge to uphold the law of the land. That Lindsey was the one being hurt challenged his moral code in a way he'd never anticipated.

When she cupped his cheek, he captured her hand, turned his face and kissed her palm. Her emotion-filled eyes were fixated on his face. His heart kicked against his chest like a horse straining to be set free.

"Silver…" Her voice was like a physical caress. No one had said his name quite like that before.

He leaned in and set his lips against hers, barely touching, testing the waters. Giving her time to react, to pull away or shove him or demand to know why he was changing the rules. She did none of those things. Lindsey slid her hand along his shoulder, her fingertips tickling his nape before splaying into his hair. Lightbulbs exploded behind his eyelids. Curving his arm around her waist, he deepened the kiss.

She smelled like vanilla and pine and earth. She was a blend of sweetness and uncertainty, as eager to be close to him as he was to her. The boss-employee barrier no longer existed. To be honest, it had blurred long ago. He shouldn't feel guilty for kissing Lindsey Snow, but he knew it wasn't the smartest move.

Silver rested his forehead against hers and tried to gather his wits. They'd been thrust into a dangerous game. He was 99 percent positive things would be very different if they weren't trying to outmaneuver a pair of killers. They might not even be on speaking terms.

He'd had more than a year with Lindsey and hadn't chosen to pursue her. He couldn't trust this new and unexpected intimacy springing up between them. He couldn't trust his own heart, and he wasn't convinced he could trust hers.

SIXTEEN

Lindsey had had a string of rotten days. With one kiss, Silver had wiped out the negative. Inside, she was squealing with girlish glee. How many times had she daydreamed about this day? Foster Williams was attracted to *her*. He'd kissed *her*. Outwardly, she was hopefully projecting a calm, cool and collected vibe.

She framed his elegant face, trailing her thumb lightly beneath the still-healing scratch on his cheek.

"I've been waiting a long time for you to do that," she murmured, feeling her cheeks heat up. *So much for playing it cool.*

In the inviting light of his living room, his eyes were a brilliant sapphire blue. He swallowed hard. Let his eyelids drift closed. "Lindsey," he whispered, his voice sounding pained.

He pulled out of the embrace and stood, raking his hands through his hair and avoiding her gaze.

Uh-oh.

He didn't seem happy. The delight fizzing through her faded. Logic dulled her elation with reminders of why he shouldn't pursue any lasting connection with her.

His alarm buzzed a notification. He frowned at his phone. "It's SPD," he stated in a solemn tone. "Here to take our statements."

He strode to the door and greeted the officers. It gave her time to mentally regroup. Her emotions were another matter. She wouldn't ever forget how it felt to be close to him, wouldn't stop longing to repeat the experience.

The officers recorded the details of their accounts. They didn't have much to offer in return, other than they'd found tire tracks and footprints on the outskirts of Silver's property and were in the process of making molds for the CSU lab. They'd return in the morning and search for the bullet the woman had discharged. If they found it, they might be able to match it to a specific gun. As soon as they left, Silver made a call to a private security firm.

"Remember Angus and Tyson?" He positioned himself across the room, between the fireplace and decorated tree, one arm propped on the mantel.

"You hired them as protection backup for Tessa and Lily."

"I'm employing their services again. They promised to be here before midnight. You can rest easy tonight."

He was keeping his distance. The message was loud and clear—he regretted his actions and wouldn't be repeating them. Lindsey's exhaustion was bone deep. She was weary and worn down and more than a little irritated with herself. How could she have forgotten, even for a moment, that a future with Silver was out of the question?

Although Silver seemed surprised when she retreated to the office, he didn't try to dissuade her. The night was a restless one. There were two people looking to end her life, and they'd come close to accomplishing their goals. Also devastating? Silver wished the kiss undone. It would've been better to continue in her futile daydreams than to experience the real thing, only to be rejected.

The next morning after a rushed breakfast, he drove her to the stables. Angus and Tyson followed in their gray sedan with blacked-out windows. The intimidating pair remained outside, guarding the entrances. The team convened in the meeting room as soon as the horses were fed.

Raven assumed the chair beside Lindsey and gave her a side hug. Her leg injury had called for a dozen stitches, but it wasn't enough to keep her out of work.

Cruz claimed the end chair, and Silver sat across from Lindsey. He'd said little in the truck, and his expression was somber.

Mason stood at the other end of the windowless rectangular room. Framed photos of mounted police units from across the state formed a mosaic against the stark white walls. He erased the writing on the whiteboard and wielded a dry-erase marker. His laptop sat open on the table.

They were all wearing dark pants and long-sleeved shirts with the Serenity Mounted Patrol emblem on the chest. Lindsey felt like a gel marker in a box of ballpoint pens. Fortunately, she hadn't lost all of her belongings in the explosion. The cabin she'd chosen to stay in at Camp Smoky had had scant storage, and she'd stored the bulk of her belongings in the cabin across from hers.

"Cruz and Raven, you're patrolling the town square today. With only eight days until Christmas, that area will be swarming with shoppers. Silver, there's been a rise in thefts in the Sunset Ridge neighborhood. Lieutenant Hatmaker asked us to patrol over there and try to get intel from the residents." His gaze flicked to Lindsey. "Are you both okay with her staying here with Angus and Tyson?"

Silver sat with his arms folded. His gaze grazed hers, his brows uplifted. "Lindsey?"

"Fine with me."

"We'll be back around noon," Mason said, closing his laptop. "Before we head out, I'd like to review where we're at with Lindsey's case. York has the lead, but he's been handed several high-profile cases this week. The attacks have moved from the camp to Silver's home base, and that's a huge concern."

"Attacking a cop's house? Bold move." Cruz scowled.

"Risky, too," Raven added. "Did we get any leads with the truck?"

"I haven't heard anything yet, other than it was stolen from a Gatlinburg resident. The plates were switched out."

"Lindsey, are you sure there's no one in your past who'd like to get even?" Twirling a pen between his fingers, Cruz leveled his penetrating gaze at her.

She reached up out of habit to straighten her glasses, only to find her nose bare. "I'm sure."

"What about an old classmate? A work colleague?" he pressed. "An ex-boyfriend? Someone from a dating site you met for coffee?"

Lindsey had racked her brain again and again for answers and had come up empty. She shook her head. "There's no one."

"Oh, there's someone all right," Cruz countered. "Someone angry enough to blow up a cabin with a cop inside."

Lindsey felt the blood drain from her face.

Silver seized Cruz's sleeve. "Leave her alone."

"I'm trying to help." He yanked free of Silver's grasp.

"We're all feeling the pressure," Mason said, his tone demanding a cease-fire. "When Tessa and I were in trouble, we knew our enemy's identity. We knew how Dante operated and could at least try to anticipate his plan. Silver and Lindsey don't have that luxury."

Cruz nudged her boot. "I meant no disrespect, Lindsey."

She summoned a smile for his sake. Cruz Castillo could be brusque in nature, but he had a heart of gold. He was also quick to acknowledge his mistakes, and she had to respect him for that.

Raven tapped her notebook with her pen. "Our perps are adaptable, proficient with various weapons and determined to carry through with their plans. I'm thinking ex-military."

Mason reviewed the highlights of the case, jotting notes and names on the board. He crossed off the Shaws, as well as repairman Norman Miller. He circled Albert Bartosz.

Lindsey made a protesting squeak. "Albert is harmless."

"I've been doing this a long time," Mason said, not unkindly. "Anyone is capable of crossing the line, given the right circumstances."

Silver shifted forward in his seat and propped his arm on the table. "Lindsey spoke to Camp Smoky's owner, Eugene Butler, yesterday. Apparently, his adult children want him to sell and split the proceeds. It's worth looking into."

"Do you know their names, Lindsey?" Raven asked.

"No, I don't."

She scooted her laptop over and began typing. "Eugene's located in Ohio, correct?" At Lindsey's nod, she continued scrolling. "Here it is—Bruce and Kayla Butler. Kayla was married to a Mike Lansing but divorced last year and began using her maiden name again. Hold on." She peered at the photos on the screen. "I recognize this guy. Cruz, remember when we were working that accident on Highway 321 last week?"

"The one with the motorcycle wrapped around the telephone pole?" He leaned into Lindsey's space for a better look. "What about it?"

"Traffic was backed up for miles. This guy, Bruce Butler, was furious. He got out of his car…" She snapped her fingers. "A maroon sedan. Buick, I think. I had to threaten him with a citation to get him to return to his vehicle."

Silver reached across the table and angled the laptop his direction. "He's a match with the man's silhouette I saw last night."

"What about Kayla?" Raven rattled off her description stats.

"I'm less sure about that one." His eyes had a determined glint to them. "Lindsey, try to get Eugene on the phone. See if he's familiar with his children's travel itineraries."

Lindsey's heart hammered against her chest. Were they finally close to the right answers, ones that would end this nightmare?

Eugene denied any knowledge of Bruce or Kayla being in Tennessee recently. After the call was concluded, Raven addressed the room.

"I did a little digging. Turns out Bruce has a couple of priors, including assault and battery."

"Kayla?"

"She's clean, as far as records indicate."

Mason contacted Dispatch and issued a BOLO for Bruce Butler. He also instructed Raven to print photos of Bruce and Kayla and show them to the shop owners while on patrol.

The officers headed to the locker room to change into their official uniforms. Lindsey followed them into the hallway and asked Silver to wait.

He motioned her into the break room. "Something wrong?"

"Do you truly think Bruce and Kayla are behind all this?"

He kneaded the back of his neck. "Money is a powerful motivator."

"Even if they got me out of the way, who's to say Eugene wouldn't hire a replacement?"

"Maybe they think property destruction and the death of his employee is enough to sway him." He sighed. "They're our only leads at the moment, and we've got to follow the trail. See where it takes us."

Lindsey wrapped her arms around her upper body, wishing he would close the gap and hold her. His warmth and strength would stave off these unsettled feelings inside her.

"Do you need anything before I go?" He gestured to the vending machines against the wall. "There's a bowl of change on my desk. Help yourself. Or there's the endless supply of coffee."

"I'm good for now."

"Angus and Tyson are right outside." His expression revealed nothing of his thoughts. "You have my number."

His detached demeanor frustrated her. She wanted to poke him in the chest. Or maybe slug his arm. Definitely stamp her feet in dismay. How could he switch gears like that? Go from tender and caring to cool and distanced? Lindsey understood that he didn't want a future with her, but he didn't have to act like she was a criminal. They could be civil. Friendly, even. She was on the verge of confronting him when she heard Raven and Cruz talking out in the stall area. Her questions would have to wait.

Silver paced the length of his bedroom later that evening, his gaze fixated on the thick file folder on the corner of his bed. He'd read through the entire stack of emails last night. After the kiss they'd shared, he could no longer resist their pull. Reading the ongoing conversation between Lindsey and his mother had been surreal and uncomfortable. He'd felt like an eavesdropper, even though *he* was the main topic. To her credit, Lindsey hadn't been as forthcoming as one might expect, especially considering she was getting compensated. As the months had marched on, she'd become even less so. Because she'd gotten to know him? To like him?

He attempted to squash the toasty, cookies-warm-from-the-oven feelings spilling through him. The fact that these emails existed was a major obstacle to any lasting relationship. He hadn't managed to have a successful, meaningful connection with anyone, let alone someone who'd willfully deceived him.

Kissing her was a mistake. His withdrawal had confused her. Hurt her, too. He could see it in her eyes, the way she watched him when she thought he wasn't aware.

He clenched his fists. His parents were ultimately to blame. If they hadn't meddled, she wouldn't be in Serenity. Maybe she wouldn't be in danger.

Silver did what he rarely did—he called his mother.

Astrid's cultured voice cut into him like a dozen stabs in the back. "Mother."

There was a significant pause. "Foster? Is that you?"

He pinched the bridge of his nose. "Do you have a minute?"

"For you, always." He could hear her hurried steps and a door closing. He pictured her in her home office at the mansion, her clothes pristine and not a hair out of place. "I'm happy you called. How are you?"

"I need to talk to you about Lindsey Snow."

"Lindsey." She sighed. "She told you, I suppose. I wish she hadn't."

"You should have." He sliced the air with his hand. "Scratch that. You shouldn't have sent her."

"You're right. She certainly wasn't worth the money we paid her. I told Gordon she wasn't made for subterfuge."

Silver couldn't believe his ears. "Why didn't you come out and ask me if I would interfere with Gordon's political aspirations? Why go to the trouble of deliberately placing someone in my life?"

"You wouldn't take my calls, remember? What other choice did we have, Foster?"

He stalked to the window and stared out at the night.

What other choice, indeed? How had he survived these self-absorbed, controlling people? How was he not a complete failure?

Thank You, Lord, for not giving up on me, for placing people in my path to serve as life rafts. You brought me out of the pit and set me on a rock.

"I've heard enough." He wasn't going to get an apology or a reconciliation. His parents weren't going to magically transform into the family he'd dreamed about as a boy. He could choose to hold on to bitterness or he could choose to move on. "Lindsey's in danger. We're having a tough time nailing down who's trying to hurt her. Do you have any ideas?"

Astrid expressed an appropriate amount of shock. No surprise, she didn't have valuable input. However, she promised to send over a list of interns and coworkers Lindsey had interacted with during her time at Williams Industrial.

Silver ended the call and considered going for a swim. He'd skipped supper, however, and the lunch he'd shared with Mason was long gone. He stored the file folder in a dresser drawer and ascended the steps. Lindsey was behind the kitchen island, arranging red-and-white flowers in a vase. She noticed his approach and shot him a tentative smile.

"Who are those from?"

"The Andersons." She turned on the faucet and let water flow into the crystal container. "The signed card is on the counter."

He read the card. "Doesn't ring a bell. But then, you're the one who handled the rental information."

"They're a retired couple from Alabama and visit every Valentine's Day. Last year, they sent a variety snack basket for Christmas."

Silver glanced at the door. "I didn't hear anyone at the door. In fact, I didn't get a notification." His phone told another story. He must've been speaking to his mother and missed it.

"I saw the delivery van outside. Tyson intercepted the driver and, after checking the items, brought them to me." She tilted her head to indicate a foil-wrapped confection box. "Check out the label. Those are expensive truffles."

Silver untied the ribbon, lifted the lid and did an inventory of the selection. "Tried one yet?"

"I got antsy alone at the stables and ate three candy bars from the vending machine. Needless to say, I've reached my sugar limit for today." She touched her nose, as if to adjust her glasses.

The optometrist in town said they could have Lindsey's replacements ready by tomorrow afternoon. She was beautiful with or without them, but he sort of preferred how the quirky glasses highlighted her eyes.

He chose the white-chocolate-ganache and dark-chocolate-hazelnut truffles. At her cocked brow, he finished chewing and shrugged. "It's been one of those days."

"It's been one of those weeks."

He was perusing the drink choices in the fridge when a call from Angus came in. "We've got a problem."

His skin prickled, and he closed the fridge. "What is it?"

"I discovered the delivery-van driver in the woods, trussed up like a Christmas goose and missing his company shirt and badge."

"Is he alive?"

"He's groggy. Has a lump on his head. He said a man waved him down as he turned into the drive, asking for directions. Next thing you know, there's a gun pointed at his face. He was made to walk into the woods and then struck from behind. He blacked out."

The flowers and chocolates drew Silver's attention, and he pointed at Lindsey. "Don't touch those again."

Her face set in worried lines, she backed away from the island.

Tyson knocked on the door, and Silver let him in. "The guy who delivered the items. What did he look like?"

"He had a cap on, so I didn't get a good look at his features. Sandy hair, blue or hazel eyes. Over six feet."

Angus promised to stay with the victim until the police arrived. Tyson advanced into the room, propped his hands on the counter and studied the chocolates with a scowl. "Who ate the truffles?"

"I did," Silver said.

Lindsey made a distressed sound and hurried to Silver's side. "You think they tampered with them?"

"They've used poison before." *Thank You, Lord, that Lindsey didn't eat any.*

Silver picked up one of the chocolates and turned it over. There, in the middle, was a tiny hole. Sweat trickled between his shoulder blades, and he flushed hot.

Lindsey learned around him for a better look and gasped.

Tyson muttered beneath his breath. "Check the rest."

Silver inspected the remaining truffles. More than half bore proof of a telltale injection site.

Lindsey seized his arm. "You have to go to the hospital."

SEVENTEEN

Lindsey resisted the urge to latch onto Silver's hand. Tyson had offered to give them a ride to the hospital, since she didn't have her glasses and Silver potentially had poison in his bloodstream. When Silver had gotten into the back seat, she'd climbed in after him. She studied his tense profile, framed by the passing scenery, and prayed nonstop.

He turned his head and met her gaze. "I feel fine," he insisted. "I'm positive I ate the nondoctored ones."

"You look pale."

"I'm always pale."

"Not like this."

She gazed deeply into his eyes. "Your pupils look normal. How's your stomach? Is your heart beating unnaturally fast?"

"My heart and stomach are the same as the last time you asked," he said patiently. "What about you? You handled the bouquet. The flowers could've been coated with a hazardous residue."

"I'm fine."

"I'll feel better if you are checked out," Silver returned.

At the hospital, they explained the situation and gave the truffles to the staff for testing. They needed to know exactly what they were dealing with. Angus had stayed behind and would let CSU inspect the flowers.

A nurse checked Lindsey's vitals and found nothing out of the ordinary. She was directed to the emergency department waiting area. Tyson stuck to her like glue while Silver was taken to a separate area for more in-depth testing.

Before long, Raven and Cruz strolled in and peppered her with questions. Mason wasn't far behind. When the guys went on a coffee hunt, Lindsey turned to her friend.

"Silver's fortunate to have you," she told Raven. In her mind, God had provided a substitute family for him.

"He's got you, too."

"If I was him, I would run far and fast. Being associated with me right now is dangerous." The futility of her situation pressed down on her. She had no control, no say, no way to keep others safe. "First Thea, then you. Silver. The delivery driver."

Raven leaned in. "None of this is your fault."

Who else was there to blame? If only she knew what she'd done to inspire these cruel actions.

"I know that look." Raven grasped her shoulder. "Don't torture yourself, Linds. Nothing you could've done would merit this type of response. So far, we've found nothing to connect this to anyone in your personal sphere."

Lindsey didn't respond, and Raven tried to distract her while they waited.

Silver emerged two hours later. "I'm good to go."

Lindsey rushed over, stopping short of throwing her arms around him. "What did they say?"

"My blood work was normal. They monitored my breathing, oxygen levels and more."

Mason tossed his empty coffee cup in the garbage. "What was in the truffles?"

"Get this—prescription eye drops."

Cruz grunted in disbelief. "What can that do?"

"Serious damage, believe or not," Silver answered.

"Dramatic rise and fall in blood pressure, seizures and even coma. In some cases, it can lead to death."

Lindsey's mouth dried. *Thank You, Lord, for protecting us both.* "Any word on the driver?"

"Already treated and released. Officer Bell got his statement before coming to see me."

Mason scraped his hand down his face. "Silver, I know you planned to be involved with Christmas for Cops again, but with things escalating…"

Disappointment flickered in his eyes. "I agree it's too risky. I'll sit this one out."

Raven's forehead bunched. "Law enforcement will be crawling over the square, though."

"These people don't care," Mason responded, anger at the situation darkening his gaze.

Lindsey hated that Silver would miss out on something that was important to him, but there was nothing she could do about it. The ride home was quiet. Angus informed them that CSU had come and gone. The private security guards were going to switch shifts with two of their co-workers for the night.

When Silver brought an entire pizza down to the office an hour later, she left the desk. "Are you sure that's safe to eat?"

"Tyson drove to the pizza place himself. It's safe."

"I'm happy to hear it, because I'm hungry enough to eat a horse." She laughed at his expression. "I guess that's not the best phrase to use around a mounted police officer." Taking the box over to the couch, she then placed it on the cushion beside her. He didn't join her, however. "Aren't you hungry?"

He rolled the desk chair over and sat, propping his arms on the rests and linking his fingers. "Lindsey, we need to talk."

Her appetite evaporated.

"Things are unsettled between us, and I wanted to clear up any confusion."

"I see."

His eyes were sad. "I like you, Lindsey. I do. You're an exceptional person—"

"But you wish we hadn't kissed," she supplied, sadness gripping her. "I understand. It won't happen again."

"I don't know that you do. If I was a different person, if I'd had a normal upbringing and wasn't cursed with trust issues, I'd be able to get past the connection between you and my parents."

"You read the emails."

He slowly nodded. "Last night."

This was worse than if he simply wasn't attracted to her or didn't like her. He was essentially saying that, if not for her duplicity, he might've pursued a relationship with her. But how would their paths have ever crossed? Either way, she wasn't going to wind up with her dream guy.

The air was thick with horse sweat and hay as Silver untacked Lightning. Non-horse people typically scrunched their noses when they entered the stables. He used to be in that category. Now he identified the smells with the satisfaction of a job well done and the rewards of having an equine partner. He'd forever be grateful for the chance to work with mounted patrol.

Mason cross-tied Scout farther down the aisle. Although their patrol had been uneventful, Silver had been on edge. His thoughts had been divided between his tasks—staying alert to trouble while interacting with citizens—and Lindsey, who'd remained at the stables. She'd made no mention of last night's conversation during breakfast or the ride here.

"You should consider taking some time off." Mason

had already removed Scout's tack and was loosening dirt using a curry brush.

Silver looped the bridle on a hook. "Is that a suggestion or a command?"

For some, working with friends might pose problems. Silver hadn't run into any issues having his best friend as a higher-ranking officer.

"You have plenty of vacation days saved up, and this is the slower season." He spoke over Scout's broad back. "You wouldn't have to leave Lindsey in the break room for hours on end."

"She hasn't complained."

He cocked his head. "She's not a complainer in general."

It was true that Lindsey had a glass-half-full outlook. The danger surrounding her had no doubt tarnished the glass a bit, but she hadn't let on.

"I don't know. Being stuck in my house 24/7..." With Lindsey. He could see several ways that scenario could deteriorate.

Mason studied him with a shrewd gaze. Thankfully, he didn't probe. "Think about it."

Lindsey emerged from the front hallway, squinting a bit as she surveyed the stalls. He didn't understand how she wasn't dealing with a constant headache. *Maybe she is, and she hasn't mentioned it.*

"Hey, Lindsey," he called. "I'll be ready to go in half an hour."

Instead of returning to the break room, she advanced toward him, a crease between her brows. Without her scarf, the pink marks left by the belt used to strangle her were visible. He averted his gaze.

"Edward called. There's a problem at the camp."

Silver walked to Lightning's other side. "Remind me who he is."

"Edward O'Connor. He and his men are remodeling the kitchen and cafeteria. He's discovered evidence of a leak, and the damage is extensive. He needs for me to come out there and discuss ways to fix it. Do you mind?"

"Tyson will accompany us, so I don't see why not."

"Thanks."

Mason stepped forward. "Want me to come, too?"

"You've got a family at home waiting for you."

"Tessa understands that life with a cop is never routine, and I won't always be home for supper." His gaze bounced between them. "I'm here in whatever capacity you need me."

"Thanks, brother."

As soon as they finished grooming the horses, they locked up the stables and apprised Tyson of the plan. Silver and Lindsey rode in the unit truck, which was sandwiched between Tyson's sedan and Mason's truck.

Silver glanced at her wan profile. She was practically hugging the passenger door, her elbow propped on the ledge and her chin in her hand. He missed her spunk, her sparkling eyes and infectious smile.

"What did you do today?"

She lifted her head. "I flipped through some magazines. I spent time with Iggy and King. Do you think they mind not being in on the action as much as the others?"

The unit had six horses. While all received the same training, Iggy and King weren't utilized in day-to-day operations. "I'm positive they're satisfied with life. We rotate them into the patrol schedule on a regular basis."

"And give them lots of attention?"

"And treats."

"I'm glad. I wouldn't want them to be jealous or feel left out."

He chuckled. "What else did you do?"

"Some online shopping. Christmas is in seven days. I prefer to shop in person, to handle and touch and smell things before I purchase. I have to get it in my head that this year will be different." She shrugged one shoulder. "I'm having the gifts delivered to my parents' house. Mom will have to wrap everything, including what I got her."

"You spent a week with them last year, right?"

"Yes." Her sigh was heavy. "Eve wasn't around. She didn't even call my parents to wish them merry Christmas. Her absence is tough on everyone, but it's easier, you know? When she's there, her sour mood permeates everything."

"Yet you still adore Christmas."

"I try not to let the bad overshadow the hope that underscores the season. Jesus Christ is the hope of the world, the bridge between sinful man and holy God. That's the true reason I love Christmas."

Her voice vibrated with that very hope she spoke about. "You have a close relationship with Him, don't you?"

Lindsey's smile brightened her entire face. "He's my best friend."

Silver wanted that intimacy with God for himself. He was tired of holding a piece of himself apart, out of God's reach. *I'm sorry, Lord, for not giving you my all. Please help me to put You first, to love You with all my heart, soul and strength. Please heal me. Take away my bitterness and help me forgive my parents, once and for all.*

The peace of confession settled into his heart, and he knew that giving his burdens to the Lord was right and good.

He turned onto the camp road behind Tyson's sedan. The dwindling daylight sent shafts of light through the trees and outlined the cabins ringing the lake. Lindsey sat up straighter and gasped aloud at the sight of the destroyed cabin.

"It looks worse than I imagined." She braced her hand on the dash. "It will have to be razed, won't it?"

"Looks that way."

Tyson parked directly in front of the cafeteria's double doors. A covered porch ran the length of the building, and there were multiple entrances. When Silver, Lindsey and Mason got out of their vehicles, Edward emerged. Silver's hackles immediately rose.

"Lindsey. Thank you for coming." He cleared his throat and licked his lips. "I didn't know you were bringing friends."

Silver and Mason exchanged a look. "Is that a problem?"

"No problem." He glanced over his shoulder.

Silver positioned himself between Edward and Lindsey. "Is there something you need to tell us?"

"I'm sorry. I didn't know what to do."

Movement registered out of the corner of his eye, and his hand went to his holster as a man and woman approached from the left. He recognized them from their photos— Bruce and Kayla Butler.

Tyson and Mason closed ranks, flanking Silver and Lindsey.

"Show your hands," Silver called.

The pair lifted their palms to the sky. "We don't want any trouble," Bruce said. "We just want to talk to Lindsey Snow."

EIGHTEEN

Lindsey shifted to get a glimpse of Edward. "Is there a leak or isn't there?"

His guilty expression said it all. "I didn't have a choice. They're the property owners. They threatened to fire me and my men if I didn't get you up here."

"They misled you," she shot back. "Their father's name is on the deed, not theirs."

Tension radiated from Silver. He kept one hand on his holster and the other as a barrier in front of her. "Bruce. Kayla. You've lured her up here. Why don't you tell Lindsey what's on your minds?"

Lindsey turned her attention to the siblings. Could they be the ones who'd accosted her on Silver's property? Bruce was brawny enough to shoulder her through the mountainous terrain. Kayla was on the petite side, but not scrawny. She had the build of an athlete. They looked like average, law-abiding citizens.

"You have to convince my father to sell." Kayla jutted forward, her arms stretching wide.

"Not another step," Silver warned, removing his weapon. He kept it angled at the ground, but the message was clear.

Her eyes rounded, then her jaw set. "He's holding on to it out of principle. He thinks selling will dishonor my mom's memory."

"That's his right," Lindsey answered. "I've spoken to Eugene at length. He has a deep fondness for this camp and many joyful memories. He plans to visit once it's restored."

Bruce rolled his eyes. "He should enjoy his last days, not dump money into this lost cause."

"What's in it for you?" Silver demanded. When neither spoke, he said, "You drove a long way to confront Lindsey in person, when a simple phone call would suffice."

Kayla's body language was defiant. "I lost my job two months ago. I've depleted my savings and haven't been able to find a new position. I'm on the verge of losing my home."

"I have three kids to put through college," Bruce said. "Dad's being unreasonable. He can't relive the glory years. He can't bring back Mom."

"But he *can* help us, in the here and now." Kayla practically shook with the forcefulness of her claim. "He needs someone connected to the camp to talk sense into him. He likes you, Lindsey. He trusts you. I know he'll listen to you. You have to try."

Lindsey could sympathize with Kayla's plight, but she didn't approve of her methods. "You should go home and discuss this with your father."

"But—"

Mason intervened, sending Edward back inside to rejoin his men and insisting the pair come to the station.

Bruce balked. "Why would we do that? We've done nothing wrong."

"It's an informal inquiry, that's all. We've had some trouble around here, as you probably noticed." Mason gestured in the vicinity of the demolished cabin. "You might've seen something useful."

Lindsey held her breath, wondering if the pair would outright refuse.

"Why can't we talk here?" Kayla asked.

"Our lead detective is waiting for us in town."

They reluctantly agreed, and Mason accompanied them to their vehicle, parked near the staff cabins. Silver's jaw unlocked and the invisible string tying his shoulder blades together snapped. He replaced his weapon in its holster and looked at her.

"You okay?"

"I'm sad for Mr. Butler. His own kids are putting their wants and needs above his, demanding their way as if they're toddlers." She watched the departing trio. "Do you think they're behind the attacks?"

"Anything is possible. I'll reserve judgment until after York's done with them."

"What should I do about Edward? If I fire him midjob, it might take weeks to find a replacement."

"Aside from today's error in judgment, do you have any other complaints?"

"None."

"He seemed remorseful. I need to be in on the interviews, so we don't have time to confront him now. You could have a phone conversation with him tonight and make sure he knows to watch his step from here on out. I'll even join the call if you want."

Lindsey thanked him, grateful for his willingness to help her in whatever capacity.

At the station, she waited in the break room until the separate interviews were finished. Officer Bell returned from patrol and, seeing her alone at the table, rustled up a hot chocolate for each of them. She knew him from church, but their paths hadn't crossed much.

When Silver returned and saw them chatting, something flashed in his eyes. He quickly subdued it. Did he dislike James Bell? Had there been some professional disagreement in their past?

"Lindsey, York wants to discuss his findings."

She followed him to a corner office, where the seasoned detective sat behind a metal desk from a bygone era. Mason stood in the corner, arms crossed, his expression frustrated. She took that to mean the interviews hadn't gone well.

When she was seated in one of the two chairs facing the desk, Silver closed the door and lowered himself onto the seat beside her.

York didn't waste time on pleasantries. "I've released the Butlers. I have no evidence linking them to the crimes against you."

Her stomach sank. "We're back to square one then."

"Not exactly. I haven't ruled out their involvement. I told them to stick around town for a few days. That will give us time to dig into their lives and hopefully get results from the stolen truck and crime scene. Whoever is after you has access to medical supplies, weapons and explosives."

"Or they have connections with access," Silver interjected.

"Or they steal it themselves." Mason pushed off the wall. "I'm inclined to believe they're culpable. Kayla's on the brink of financial ruin. Money troubles can push reasonable people over the edge."

"Would they confront me, though? Wouldn't they want to avoid suspicion?"

York used his foot to swivel his chair side to side, the wheels in his head obviously turning. "Maybe they think that by coming out into the open, they've ceased being suspicious."

She angled toward Silver, her knee bumping his. "You saw my attackers in the woods."

"It was dark. My adrenaline was pumping, the dogs were going crazy and I was laser focused on saving you."

Those first moments of consciousness scrolled through

her mind like a full-color movie. He'd called her *honey*. Tenderly touched her face, brushed her hair aside. That was the night he'd kissed her.

"Tyson can't make a positive ID, either," Mason added. His voice pulled her back to the present.

Why couldn't they seem to catch a break? By the time they figured out her enemies' identities, she'd be 100 percent in love with Silver Williams, and there'd be no remedy.

"I'm not happy that others are sick." Lindsey emerged from the truck the next evening, tucked the lapels of her coat closer together and smiled up at him, her lips cherry red against her white teeth. "But I am glad you aren't going to miss out on this event. Last year, you talked about it for days afterward."

Silver shared her feelings. Mason had called earlier in the day, explaining that several of the sheriff's department guys had come down with the flu. If they didn't have enough officers, they would have to cancel Christmas with Cops. Silver had hired extra private security guards, allowing Tyson to watch over Lindsey while Angus tailed Silver and his young shopping partner.

"I wish you could come shopping with us," he said. "The kids are a blast. Some are shy and need coaching. Others need help reining in their enthusiasm."

"If I remember correctly, you said their reticence doesn't last once the party starts. I'll be there helping with setup and trying not to eat all the sugar cookies."

Silver reached out and freed a lock of hair that had gotten twisted in her dangly earring. Her shiny hair framed her face, which seemed to glow in the lamp light. They'd picked up her glasses last night after leaving the station, and the printed frames enhanced her warm brown eyes.

She gazed up at him with unabashed affection and longing, and he felt mirroring emotions surge through him. It was going to be more difficult than he'd imagined to cut her out of his life. But it was necessary. He couldn't pursue whatever this was brewing between them and risk them both getting hurt. He wasn't going to demand she leave Serenity again, but he knew it was for the best. They needed a clean break. He'd even help her find a new job in Nashville.

Tyson walked up behind them, his breath forming clouds in the air. "Ready?"

Silver glanced around the parking lot adjacent to the library and courthouse. The old-fashioned streetlamps emitted white halos of light that did little to dispel the shadows. He knew better than to loiter out in the open. He'd gotten distracted—a common occurrence around Lindsey.

He placed his hand on the small of her back, and they walked together toward the square. Shops were laid out in an even grid around a central parklike area with trees, brick pathways, benches and a fountain. During the holiday season, craft vendors assembled around the square, selling everything from crocheted cats to candles, hot-chocolate bombs and ornaments. There were food vendors, as well, and the aromas of caramel popcorn and freshly brewed coffee swirled around them.

Officer Weiland and Lieutenant Hatmaker saw them and waved. Tyson pointed out his coworkers who, like him and Angus, were in plain clothes.

"You spent a lot of time down here last December, didn't you?" he asked.

Lindsey nodded, her gaze darting from one booth to another, like a kid trying to soak in the pile of presents on Christmas morning. "I purchased ornaments to distribute among your guests. With your permission, of course."

He remembered the night she'd returned to his house, radiating excitement, her arms full of her purchases. She'd deposited them on his dining table and showed him each design. Silver had been bemused, not sure why something so simple, something she wasn't keeping for herself, would bring her such joy. But that was Lindsey. She enjoyed giving to others and making them happy.

In the large field between the square and the main highway, a giant white tent with plastic windows and pointy peaks had been set up. It was where the officers, kids and civilian volunteers would gather at the end of the night for food, games and gifts.

Silver accompanied her inside the tent, which had been transformed into a winter wonderland. A parquet floor had been installed, along with round tables draped in sparkly cloths. White, green and pink decorated trees were placed around the rectangular space, with wrapped gifts beneath each one. Heaters kept the chill at bay.

The small army of volunteers put Lindsey to work sorting out the dessert station.

"This was either the best idea or the worst," he said, smiling.

She removed her coat, revealing a sparkly gold sweater that complemented her hair and eyes.

"I am able to practice restraint," she quipped, her eyes dancing. "Unless it's peanut butter and chocolate. That I can't resist."

"I have to go. Keep an eye on her, Tyson."

Tyson's watchful demeanor didn't falter. Silver hadn't seen him crack a smile, but he wasn't paying him for his personality.

Angus was waiting for Silver outside the tent entrance. They made their way to the far end of the field, near Candace Reed's day care. Mason, Raven and Cruz separated from the crowd and joined him. Like Silver, they were in their winter uniforms and thick black jackets.

"Glad you could make it," Raven said, slapping him on the back. "Lindsey's in the tent?"

"At the dessert station, of all places."

"Now that's dangerous," Cruz wisecracked, shaking his head.

When the kids arrived, excited chatter filled the night air. Silver was paired with a towheaded boy of ten named Isaac. The boy was quiet and uncertain, so Silver set about making him comfortable. By the time they entered the second shop, Isaac was relaxed and smiling.

He wished Lindsey could be with them. She would've made the experience that much better. Truth be told, she made everything better.

The thought startled him. Was what he felt for Lindsey more serious than he'd realized?

NINETEEN

This had been the best night of the season. Certainly the best since Thea had been hurt, and Lindsey had been forced to face the specter of an unknown killer. For a few hours, she had pushed her predicament to the back of her mind and enjoyed serving the kids. Her attention drifted to the entrance, to where Silver was shaking hands with Isaac. Putting the last of the leftover cookies in the box, she hurried over to say goodbye.

After the kids and adults had gone through the line, her dessert-station partner had urged her to grab a plate and join in the festivities. She'd gotten to sit with Silver and his young charge, and the rapport between the officer and boy had made her happy and sad. He'd make a wonderful father someday. She glanced around, wondering which fortunate woman would earn his trust and love.

"Good night, Isaac," she told him, handing him an extra candy cane. "Merry Christmas."

His smile stretched from ear to ear. "Thank you, Miss Lindsey."

As soon as he'd gone, a gusty sigh whooshed from Silver. "Great kid. He's new this year. He told me about his mom, that she struggles to balance two jobs while raising him and his sister." His brows pulled together, and his eyes got a far-off look.

"You're wondering what more you can do to help, aren't you?"

He shot her a look of appeal. "You're no longer my employee, but you're resourceful. Would you consider working together to formulate a plan?"

"Of course. I'd like that."

His smile had a tender quality she hadn't seen before, and it made her eyes well up. Turning away, she motioned to the cleanup underway. "I'm going to help."

Tyson remained beside the food tables, a watchful statue apart from the activity. His gaze never seemed to stop moving. Occasionally, he would receive a text or phone call, but he didn't allow himself to be distracted for long.

The officers assisted the event volunteers in stacking chairs and folding tables. Silver and Cruz hefted the growing number of garbage bags outside while Lindsey repacked ornaments.

Tyson appeared at her side. Beneath the brim of his tweed newsboy hat, his gray eyes were solemn—that seemed to be his default mode.

"The garbage receptacles are full. They had to take them to the courthouse. We're to meet Silver at the truck."

Lindsey had thought they would stay until everyone went home. Maybe something had spooked Silver. Or maybe he was exhausted. He'd been juggling his unit responsibilities with her protective detail.

"I'll get my coat."

He held it up.

"Oh, thanks."

She shrugged into the sleeves. Before she'd finished fastening the buttons, Tyson began striding toward the back entrance used for carting out the supplies. Again, she didn't question him, although she was surprised at his haste.

Lindsey said goodbye to the volunteers she passed, hurrying to catch up. He stopped and held the flap open for her. They walked past the parked rental-company trucks. The cold squeezed its bony hand around her, and she fished her gloves from her pocket and tugged them on. The temperature had dropped dramatically since the party's start.

She concentrated on navigating the field in the dark, not on which direction they were headed. Then the lights grew dimmer, and she looked up and saw trees and the boat-and-bike-rental shop ahead, boarded up for the season. Tyson had led her behind the main shopping area. She could see the rear exterior of Spike's and other shops in that strip.

"Why did we come this way?"

"It's faster." He took hold of her arm, a little too tightly for comfort.

Apprehension crawled down her spine. She was unable to discern his expression or gauge his intent. Surely, he wouldn't betray a client or his employer.

She shortened her strides. Tyson practically propelled her into the copse.

"Let go." Lindsey tried to contain her growing panic.

He whipped her around, twisting her ankle in the process. She cried out. He shoved her against the nearest tree. There was a ripping sound, and his fingers pushed tape over her mouth, grinding her lips against her teeth.

Lindsey writhed, tripping over his leg and falling to the twig-infested ground. They poked and pricked at her through her coat and pants. Before she could remove the tape and scream for help, he bound her ankles and wrists. Then he hoisted her over his muscle-swollen shoulder and marched toward the rental shop.

Every step was a jarring bounce. There was a rushing

sound in her ears, and she felt certain she was going to lose consciousness. How could she possibly escape? Tyson was a former navy SEAL. He was also three times her size.

Why would he want her dead?

Lindsey's confusion turned to horror when he stopped and turned, and she caught sight of the water. Glory Pond. The stars overhead glistened on the placid surface. Was he going to tie a concrete block around her ankle and sink her to the bottom? Place her in a body bag and roll her in?

A rumble broke the silence. She couldn't see what was in front of Tyson, but she pictured a motorcycle or off-road vehicle. The engine quit. A seat squeaked.

"Got my money?" Tyson demanded.

There was no vocal response, only the thud of something hitting the ground, then a slow slide.

"Open it up. I want to see the cash before I give you the woman."

She heard a click. Tyson was apparently satisfied with what he saw, because he walked forward and slung her down, shoving her onto a rear-facing seat. She tried to cry out, to protest. His eyes became angry slits, and he seized her chin and thrust her head against a metal bar.

"Make another sound, and I'll knock you out." When she just stared at him, dumbfounded by this about-face in his manner, he growled, "Understand?"

She nodded as best she could, and he released her. Her phone began to buzz. Silver. He must've already noticed her absence and was searching for her. Hope seeped into her veins.

Tyson heard it, too. He jammed his hand into her coat pocket, removed the phone and, after crushing it with his boot, tossed it into the pond.

He guided her bound hands to the handrail by the bench. "Hold on. You're going for a long ride."

Tyson patted the top of the off-road vehicle, and it jerked into motion. Something cold, hard and round dug into the side of her neck. A gun.

"Don't even think about jumping."

A male's voice. Bruce Butler? She couldn't tell. She could hardly think as they bumped over the terrain, leaving Glory Pond and the rental shack behind. Tyson disappeared into the copse.

What was his plan? Flee with the cash?

Or would he hide it, return to the party and pretend innocence?

As they skirted the outer edge of a campground closed for the season, Lindsey wondered who had managed to convince Tyson to betray her. And what would this stranger do with her once they reached their destination?

Silver clenched his phone as he tried Lindsey a second time. The call went straight to voice mail.

"Something's wrong," he said, frustration slicing through him.

"Maybe she went to the restroom." Mason's gaze followed Raven and Cruz as they spoke to the remaining volunteers and officers inside the tent. "I'll check there."

Silver followed Mason outside and almost collided with Angus. "Have you seen Tyson or Lindsey? They're not inside, and neither one is answering their phone."

It was clear from his response that he thought it suspect, as well. "Let me try him. Then I'll summon the others. Someone had to have seen something."

Silver paced back and forth, scanning the square and shops, praying Lindsey had cajoled her guard to accompany her to the craft booths. Most of the vendors were in the process of packing up for the night, however.

When Angus couldn't reach Tyson, he sent out a group text to the other guards.

"How well do you know Tyson?" he demanded.

The guard's chin jutted. "I've worked with him for over three years. He's as solid as they come."

Silver had encountered solid, law-abiding people who'd compromised their morals given the right set of circumstances.

"He's responsible for Lindsey's safety when I'm not around." He clenched and unclenched his fists. "So where is he? Why isn't he able to be reached?"

Raven emerged from the tent, her gaze troubled. "Someone saw Tyson and Lindsey exit out the back, where the trucks are parked. There's no sign of them."

Silver glared at Angus. "Why would he take her that way?"

"I'm telling you, there's no way Tyson is involved in anything underhanded."

Mason jogged over. "Restrooms are vacant."

He closed his eyes and sent up a desperate prayer.

"We'll organize a search party," Mason said.

Raven summoned the officers from inside the tent. As soon as the rest of the private security guys had reached them, Mason apprised the group of their problem. Silver felt as if he was having an out-of-body experience. He couldn't concentrate because he kept picturing her in the hands of her killers, frightened out of her mind.

He was scanning the surrounding areas when a figure separated from the shadows. As soon as he recognized the burly guard, he broke into a run.

"Where is she?" he called out.

Tyson held up his hands and shook his head. As Silver got closer, he saw the bloody gash on his forehead and welts on his cheek.

"They took her," he said, panting. "We were ambushed."

Silver's heart turned to stone. "Who took her? Where?"

Tyson pointed behind him, in the direction of the parking lot and library. "A man and woman, both wearing masks. They pushed her into an SUV and took off toward the high school."

Mason and the others reached them. Cruz got in Tyson's face. "We were disposing of the garbage in plain view of the parking lot. I didn't see you or Lindsey."

Tyson was sweating profusely, and he winced as he cradled his bruised hand. "We didn't get as far as the parking lot. They got to us as we walked past Spike's."

"Why take the deserted path?" Cruz demanded. "Why leave without telling anyone?"

"Lindsey said she'd had too much punch and had to beeline it to the bathroom. We were closer to the rear entrance, so we slipped out." His eyes narrowed. "What are you trying to insinuate, Officer?"

Raven put her hand on Cruz's chest. "Let's all take a breath, okay? Finding Lindsey is our priority."

"She's right," Silver said. He had his own suspicions about the guard, but grilling him would create a delay. "What's the make and model of the SUV? I'll put out a BOLO."

Tyson rattled off the information, and Silver called it in. Mason took charge of the search, and half of the officers and private guards spread out on foot and the other half took to the roads.

"Cruz and I will cover the woods and fields around Glory Pond," Raven stated, taking out her police-issue flashlight.

Mason turned to Silver. "We'll get my truck and search around the schools."

Silver agreed without a word, feeling like his mind was

coated in ice. All he could do was pray and ask God to protect and comfort Lindsey.

Mason blasted the heater inside his truck and pulled onto the street. He didn't offer empty promises or weak platitudes. Neither spoke as they scoured the streets, sidewalks and parking lots.

"Whoever took her didn't stick around," Silver forced out. "We both know it."

"Don't let your mind go there, brother."

The mountains rose above them like hulking giants. If her captors crossed into the national park, Lindsey may not ever be located—alive or dead. The acid churned in his stomach.

"She doesn't deserve this. You should know I've forgiven her. That one act doesn't define her."

Mason spared him a quick, evaluating glance. "Smart man."

He shifted on the seat, tugging at the seat belt that felt too tight. The thoughts he'd had earlier that night about cutting her out of his life seemed ludicrous now. He'd always want to know she was okay. Safe. Thriving. Happy.

Another ten minutes passed without a sighting. "We should return to the square and question witnesses. Or start knocking on doors in these neighborhoods."

"Let's start with the square."

As Mason was turning the truck around, Raven called. He put it on speaker.

"We found an earring near the south end of Glory Pond. Wasn't Lindsey wearing gold earrings studded with miniature stars?"

Silver had a flash of their arrival, when he'd untangled her hair from the dangly earring. "That's hers."

Mason's foot got heavy on the gas. "We're on our way."

"You know what this means," he said through clenched teeth. "Tyson lied to us."

The guard had deliberately pointed them in the wrong direction, causing them to lose precious time. His involvement might've signed Lindsey's death certificate.

TWENTY

Lindsey lost count how many times she almost toppled off the seat. If not for her captor's gun, she would've already jumped. But with her ankles taped together, she couldn't run away. She didn't want to risk his wrath and earn a bullet before her time.

Face it, Lindsey. Your time is short.

Denial swept through her. She wasn't done yet. She had to at least *try* to stay alive.

Her gaze landed on her sparkly gold shoe, and inspiration struck. It was a long shot, but leaving a trail for someone to find was all she had.

She was able to get one shoe off, and it landed in the grass beside a gravel campsite. The cart swung to the right, and they passed a group of glamping tents. When they began climbing a hill, she left the other shoe.

As utter darkness closed in, and they entered isolated land, Lindsey toyed with the idea of jumping. The farther they got from town proper, the less likely she'd make it out alive. The open terrain wasn't a good option—nowhere to hide. But if they encountered woods, she could possibly roll out of sight and conceal herself.

God, I need an injection of courage. I'm not sure what the right move is. I'm scared.

The thought of never seeing her family again was heart-wrenching. And what about Silver? He'd started out as this intriguing mystery, more of an idea than anything. When she'd begun working for the flesh-and-blood man, she'd learned his quirks, preferences and habits. She'd seen that he wasn't anything like his parents. He wasn't driven to obtain more stuff, more power, more influence. He was motivated by the desire to serve others, to help those in need, to improve his community. He didn't hoard his blessings for himself. To top it off, he was the most handsome man in the world.

He occupied every corner of her heart.

A rogue tear escaped, and she gritted her teeth. Crying could wait.

She studied their surroundings as they whizzed past. Time passed in slow motion. When they finally entered the woods, she almost cried out in triumph. Biding her time was a challenge. She was impatient to get away from this silent ogre. She had no intention of meeting his female cohort, either.

When she spotted a sizable gap in the trees to her left, Lindsey let go of the bar and propelled herself off the vehicle. The landing was rougher than expected. The unforgiving earth felt like a pallet of bricks against her flesh. Air whooshed from her lungs. Something pointy penetrated her thigh, and she bit her tongue to keep from making a sound.

Her momentum pulled her downhill, rolling like a barrel, faster and faster until she slammed into a wide stump. Fingers of pain radiated from her lower back, and she almost lost her supper right then and there. Her head throbbed. Her thigh ached. But she wasn't in a stranger's clutches.

She managed to rip the tape off her mouth.

Up above, the engine cut off, and she heard foul words

spewed into the night. A thin beam swept the woods as he came searching for her.

Stay put and as silent as possible? Or try another roll downhill?

"Where is she?" Silver seized Tyson's jacket lapels.

"I told you—"

"How do you explain her earring by the pond? The fresh tire tracks?"

"What did you do?" Cruz demanded. "Have them rough you up? Or did you do it to yourself?"

"You're out of your mind," Tyson responded. But he lacked the conviction of someone falsely accused.

Mason tugged on Silver's arm. "He's not going anywhere until we see this through. We have to follow these tracks."

Silver reluctantly released him, pointing his finger at Angus's shuttered face. "Don't let him leave this spot."

Officer Bell stepped closer. "I'll make sure he doesn't."

Closer to the pond, where several flashlights were focused, Raven rose from a crouched position. "They would've gone off road. We need the horses."

They could cover more ground, and they'd have a higher vantage point from their saddles. Although his first instinct was to charge into the night, Silver accepted this was the right call.

A half-dozen patrol officers went ahead on foot, scouring the field for more clues. The stables weren't far from the square. Everyone was subdued as they readied their mounts, grabbed extra gear and headed out. He tried not to dwell on the ticking clock. He tried to approach this as any other search-and-rescue mission. He even attempted to retreat into that barren, numb place he'd accessed as a teen. He failed at all three.

When the message came through the radio that they'd found a golden shoe, his heart kicked into a gallop. He nudged Lightning's flank, and the horse responded instantly. The wind whipped at his exposed skin. At the campground, he confirmed the shoe was hers with a silent nod.

Mason inclined his head toward the hills beyond the property. "We're on the right track."

He and Mason assumed the lead, and Raven and Cruz took up the rear. Near the base of the first hill, the flashlight passed over another shiny object. Mason dismounted and retrieved it.

Her other shoe. Had she deliberately left a trail?

The blast of a rifle ricocheted off the slopes, and his heart almost stopped.

While Mason got on the radio and requested backup, Lightning responded to Silver's body language and surged toward the sound. The rest followed, and the ground reverberated with the strike of horses' hooves. He heard three more rifle shots and flinched with each one, praying the bullets wouldn't find their target.

As they crested a rise, he caught sight of an off-road golf cart's taillights. Parked at an angle near a steep drop-off, its headlights created parallel beams—enough for him to pick out the figure of a man in a green coat, holding a rifle.

Silver tugged on the reins and removed his gun from his holster.

"Police! Put down your weapon!"

The man dropped the rifle and fled into the darkness.

"I'll get him!" Cruz swept past on his horse, Renegade.

Raven and Thorn thundered after them, while Silver and Mason instructed their mounts to enter the woods. They called Lindsey's name as they descended into the cove. No response came. His flashlight failed to pick out anything useful.

Where was she?

Mason brought his mount to a complete stop and held up his hand. Silver did likewise. For long minutes, there was only silence. And then he heard her voice.

He dismounted and clambered down, using trees he passed as braces to slow his progress. "Lindsey? Talk to me."

"Over here."

She sounded winded. Hurt. He swung around the stout pine and almost tripped over her. Going to his knees, he skimmed her body with his light. "Have you been shot?"

"N-no." Her teeth were chattering. "I think my leg's injured slightly. A-And my back hurts. My head, too."

He used his knife to free her hands and feet, then unzipped his jacket and placed it over her. "Did you fall?"

"I jumped from the vehicle and rolled down. A tree stopped me more than once. I just kept propelling myself down."

He used his radio to summon EMS.

"I can walk out if you help me," she said.

"You're going to have to ride the backboard," he said, latching onto her gloved hand. "And undergo tests. Are you experiencing any numbness?"

"I can feel every little scrape and bruise—."

"That's a good sign."

Mason walked down to their location. "Lindsey, can you tell us what happened?"

"Tyson tricked me. I knew something was off, but I ignored the warnings."

"I trusted him, too," Silver told her. "We'll get answers—I promise."

"Did you get a good look at the driver?" Mason asked.

"I didn't see him. He spoke only once. I—I'm not sure if it's Bruce Butler or not."

Their radios chirped. When Silver heard that Cruz had the perp in custody, he closed his eyes and thanked God for His provision and protection.

"Is it Butler?" Mason asked.

Cruz replied in the negative. The guy didn't have ID on him, either.

Silver stayed with Lindsey while Mason and the horses rendezvoused with the others.

"What if he refuses to talk?" Lindsey said. "What if he won't give up his partner?"

"We'll find a reason for him to talk. With the charges he's facing, he'll jump on a deal offer."

Silver tucked the coat more securely around her. He'd like nothing more than to hold her, to reassure himself that she was alive and well. The past hour had taken years off his life. When EMS arrived, they quickly got her secured and ready for transport. Silver promised to meet her there as soon as he got Lightning back to the stables.

Mason clapped him on the shoulder. They were the last ones on the mountain. Cruz and Raven had taken the perp down to the campground and transferred him into the patrol unit's custody.

"How are you holding up?"

"I'm not far from coming apart."

"We're going to lean on this guy. Tyson, too. We'll learn the woman's identity and plaster her face on every billboard and bombard social media."

He leaned into Lightning and curled his arm beneath the horse's neck. "I don't know how you got through it, not only keeping Tessa safe, but Lily, too."

"It wasn't easy. There were times I had to focus on getting through one hour at a time. But I had you, Raven and Cruz, not to mention my mom and Candace." He sighed.

"Trials force us to face the truth—our own strength isn't enough. God has to be the ultimate source."

"My faith has been tested through this."

Forgiving Lindsey. Releasing his childhood pain to the Lord for healing. Leaning on God and trusting Him to work things out for his good.

"What are you going to do about Lindsey?"

"I have no idea."

He couldn't think about a future that wasn't certain or even promised. He couldn't untangle his emotions or make decisions while a killer was still on the loose. They would both end up with regrets, the kind that left lifelong scars.

TWENTY-ONE

Lindsey dragged her spoon through the neon gelatin, the tip scraping against the tray.

"You haven't eaten much today."

Silver lounged against the heater unit, his arms crossed over his chest. He was in uniform, only he'd removed the outer shirt and draped it on the chair. A long-sleeved black cotton shirt molded to his lithe upper body and thick biceps. He'd run his fingers through his hair so much that it lay flat against his head. He looked younger, but the controlled intensity oozing from his pores projected a formidable air.

"I'm not hungry."

Concern flickered in his eyes. "The nurse suggested you'd be released this afternoon. You'll rest better at home, and your appetite will return."

Lindsey didn't point out that she didn't exactly have a home here in Serenity. She'd given up her apartment for a staff cabin, which had been blown to bits. Silver's home was a temporary layover. At some point, she'd gather her meager belongings and leave. It would be as if she'd never been there.

Thinking about leaving—Silver and Serenity—deepened her gray mood to black. Maybe it was the close call, the pain medications or the fact that both suspects were hiding behind lawyers, but her hope and inherent optimism were flagging.

Lord Jesus, You see my struggle. I'm grateful You rescued me, I truly am. I'm thankful for friends who've stuck by me, despite my mistakes.

Another wave of tears crested. Her emotions had been all over the place today. She kneaded her forehead in a vain attempt to combat the dull ache there.

There was activity outside the door. Silver straightened, his hand hovering near his waist. As soon as he saw the elegant lady who entered, his jaw sagged. "Gram, what are you doing here?"

Hedda accepted his hug with an indulgent smile. "Surely you didn't think I'd stay away when you told me Lindsey had been hurt." After setting a vase containing a red, white and green arrangement on the rolling table, she came and stood beside the bed.

"Foster told me what you've been going through." She patted Lindsey's arm. "How long do you have to stay?"

"I should be released later today." She gestured to the flowers. "Thank you. They're beautiful."

"She has deep bruising on her lower back," Silver said, taking his place beside Hedda. "She has a puncture wound on her leg that will need some babying. Otherwise, she has minor cuts and bruises."

"No broken bones?"

"Not a one." Silver smiled down at Lindsey, and it was edged with pride. "Gram, Lindsey deserves a commendation. She's incredibly brave."

Bravery hadn't fueled her actions. Desperation had. "Things could've gone a different way, if not for you and the others. You found me before he could finish me off."

Silver's expression turned stark, and she regretted her choice of words.

"The Lord had other plans, my dear." Hedda turned to her grandson. "I'll be happy to stay at your house and help you care for her."

"The danger isn't over, Gram. I appreciate the offer, but I've got this."

Before Lindsey could point out that she could take care of herself, more visitors arrived. Mason and Raven walked in looking as if they hadn't slept all night.

While Mason greeted Hedda, Raven approached Lindsey's bed from the other side and leaned in for a hug.

"You were a trouper, my friend," she murmured, her eyes troubled. "How are you feeling?"

"Sore and cranky."

She cracked a half smile. "You're allowed to be cranky."

"Where are we in the case? Do we know anything about the accomplice?"

Raven shook her head and straightened. "Mason, I'll leave it to you to update them."

Hedda gripped her purse strap. "I'll wait in the hallway."

Raven introduced herself and suggested they get coffee in the cafeteria, and Hedda agreed. Before they left, Hedda patted Lindsey's hand again.

"I'll be praying for you."

Lindsey smiled her thanks, touched that Hedda had taken the time to visit her. If things were different, Silver's grandmother might've become her family. Her heart spasmed painfully.

When the door clicked shut, Mason scraped his hand along his jaw, scooted the chair closer to the bed and sat down.

"It's not good, is it?"

His brown eyes were careful in his handsome face. "We haven't made as much progress as we'd like, but we're only in the beginning stages."

"What do we know so far?" Silver said, resting his hands on his hips. He'd discarded his gloves sometime in the night and didn't seem to mind others seeing his bare hands.

"Angus was right in the sense that Tyson has nothing of note in his past. He's clean. We're digging into his family connections. Something dire must've triggered his sudden need for cash."

"Have you found the money?" Lindsey asked.

"Not yet. We've got the area around Glory Pond cordoned off and officers searching. We do have a name for the driver. Miles Downing. Does that ring a bell?"

She smoothed the paper-thin sheets over her. "I don't know anyone by that name."

"He's from the Nashville area."

"Think, Lindsey," Silver said, his voice laced with frustration. "Could Miles be a friend of an ex-boyfriend? Someone you went to university with? A fellow intern?"

She closed her eyes, but concentrating made her headache worse. "I'm sorry. There's no one."

"This guy has a colorful list of priors," Mason said. "Everything from robbery to aggravated assault. He's been in and out of jail since his teens. I can't see a connection to her college or work."

Silver thrust his hands through his hair. "Any known associates?"

"We're working on it."

"He hasn't given up anything?"

"Not yet. York discovered that Downing has a younger brother who's doing time in a Memphis-area prison. If we can somehow work out perks for the brother, Downing might agree to talk." He radiated sympathy. If anyone understood what they were going through, it was him. "You should go home and rest. Let us worry about the case."

Silver's brilliant purple-blue gaze probed hers. "I'm

tempted to use my vacation days and take her to a remote island until this is solved."

Lindsey's face probably reflected her startled surprise, because Mason ducked his head to hide a smile.

"At any rate, you're going to be relegated to the house," Silver said. "You're going to get sick of me."

Sick of him? Not likely. She lowered her gaze, hoping he didn't see the truth.

Silver left Mason with Lindsey to go in search of Gram. He couldn't believe what had come out of his mouth. A trip with Lindsey Snow? The prospect wouldn't have crossed his mind a month ago. The truth? He could spend time with her in any setting and be content.

He punched the elevator button and shook the images from his head. On the main floor, he found his grandmother preparing to leave. Raven waved goodbye and said she was going back to Lindsey's room.

"Thanks for coming, Gram. It meant a lot to her. To both of us."

She patted his cheek as if he was still that unruly, emotionally lost teenager. "You care about her. That makes her important to me, as well."

"Gram—"

"Remember, dear, we made a pact when you came to live with me."

He nodded. "To always be honest with each other, no matter what."

"Yes."

"You want honest?" he scraped out. "I'd be devastated if something were to happen to her."

I think I'm falling for her.

Silver couldn't say those words out loud. What did he know about loving someone? He loved Gram, and he loved and respected Mason, Raven and Cruz. But romantic love? The kind that led to wedding vows and sharing a home and—his heart quailed—kids?

Besides, how could they build a life together if he couldn't forget her duplicity?

"Have you told her?"

"There's nothing to tell." At her uplifted brows, he added, "I haven't figured things out for myself yet. If I do, I'll talk to her."

Gram's love for him shone brightly on her face. If not for her wisdom, limitless patience and intercessory prayer on his behalf, he wasn't sure where he'd be today.

"Do me a favor. Don't let your parents' actions rob you of happiness."

Silver hugged her. "I'll walk you to your car."

Outside, the day was bleak and blustery. The tips of the pine trees swayed to the tune of a stiff wind. Although he'd left his jacket in the room upstairs, he waited by the entrance until she pulled onto the road. His mind was full of their conversation as he passed the gift shop and information desk. Cutting by a side hall, he spotted a familiar figure and stopped short.

What was Lindsey doing down here? And in those clothes? Since when did she wear camouflage and military-style boots?

"Lindsey?"

She ducked her head, her short dark hair sliding forward to hide her profile. Pivoting, she walked quickly in the opposite direction. Silver followed, his adrenaline spiking. A terrible suspicion pulsed through him.

When he'd closed the distance between them, he lunged forward and grabbed her arm.

She whipped around, her big brown eyes skewering him with loathing. He instantly recoiled. Seeing Lindsey's features draped in ugly, hateful emotions jarred him to the core. He belatedly noticed the myriad scars on her face and neck.

"Eve?"

Her mouth twisted into a disdainful grimace. She struck out, clipping his chin with her fist and ripping free of his hand.

Rocked by the discovery, he didn't immediately pursue her. By the time his shock wore off, he'd lost her to the hospital's labyrinth of corridors.

Silver retraced his steps with increasing trepidation. How was he going to tell Lindsey?

TWENTY-TWO

"Are you comfortable?" Silver chose another plaid blanket from the basket on the hearth. He'd been hovering around her since they returned to his house. "Warm enough?"

"You've already constructed a cocoon around me," Lindsey said, studying his face.

He hadn't been acting like himself since saying goodbye to Hedda. He'd returned to the hospital room and announced she was being released, then conducted a private discussion with Mason and Raven out in the hallway. When she'd questioned him, he'd brushed aside her concerns.

He let the blanket slip from his fingers and slide into a heap atop the neatly folded stack. That wasn't his way of doing things. He returned everything to its proper place.

He gestured to the kitchen. "Are you hungry? I can fix you a grilled cheese. I don't have the sour green apples you like to eat with it, but—"

"I know what you're having trouble telling me."

His eyes got wide, and he lowered his arm to his side. "You do?"

"I've overstayed my welcome. Anyone would be tired of babysitting me, at this point. You're ready to resume your normal routine. Have your home to yourself again."

She started to push the blankets away and winced. Any movement caused her lower back to twinge, even with the pain medication she was taking. "I can rent a hotel room. I won't come out until the case is solved."

His expression turned so solemn that she almost offered him a hug.

"I'm not upset, Silver. I'm grateful for everything you've done."

"Lindsey, honey, that's not it."

Honey? He only used the endearment when the situation was dire.

He moved between the couch and coffee table, assuming a spot on the rectangular table, careful not to bump her knees with his.

"When was the last time you spoke to Eve?"

The question threw her. "Um, I'm not sure. Months, I guess. Why?"

"I saw her at the hospital."

"That's unlikely. She wants nothing to do with me. Plus, my family didn't know I was there."

She'd kept most of the facts from them. What could they do besides worry? Or rush here and try to fix things, possibly getting hurt in the process?

"I was as close to her as I am to you right now." He had a pained expression, and the reason for his strange mood became clear.

"You don't think…" Seared to the core, Lindsey shoved the blankets onto the cushion beside her. "That's preposterous! She can't be Downing's accomplice. She's my *sister*."

He leaned forward and cupped her knees. "York, Mason and the others are looking for a connection between Eve and Downing. According to Mason, Downing's reaction to the news of her sighting is suspect."

"No, this isn't right."

She stood up too fast and gasped, both her thigh and back protesting. Silver was upright in a second, his arm around her and his other hand on her waist. His chest filled her vision. She longed to seek solace in his embrace.

"I'm fine." She pushed him away.

He held his hands up, palms out. "Lindsey, please. I know this is difficult, but hear me out. You said yourself that Eve hasn't come to terms with her accident. She's nursed a lifetime of bitterness. She's made a physical and emotional break with you, her twin, as well as the rest of your family."

Denial roared through her. "You're accusing her of attempted murder, Silver."

"I pray I'm wrong," he said softly. His eyes were dark navy, full of compassion and entreaty.

Lindsey kneaded her forehead, trying desperately to sift through her tormented thoughts. Silver wasn't the enemy. He was merely the bearer of disturbing speculation.

"I need to lie down."

"Do you want the television on? Music?"

She forced her gaze to his, and she almost wept at his gentle expression. "Not here. Downstairs."

He paused. "Want me to bring you anything?"

Lindsey pressed her lips together and shook her head. He walked with her to the elevator. The dogs left their spots by the fireplace and padded behind him. She almost changed her mind. He was right there, offering friendship, comfort and solace. Instead, she chose to close herself in the office.

Lowering herself carefully into the cushioned desk chair, she called her mom.

"Lindsey, you sound exhausted."

"The past week has been stressful," she conceded. "Mom, when was the last time you heard from Eve?"

"A long time." Weariness crept into her voice. "Why? Did you talk to her? Is she in trouble?"

"This is important, Mom. What did she say exactly?"

"Not much. She quit her job at the coffee shop. Apparently, she had a disagreement with the manager, and she was angry when the owner didn't back her up."

"Does the name Miles Downing mean anything to you?"

"No."

The tension inside Lindsey's chest uncoiled.

Her mom continued, "She was enthusiastic about a new boyfriend. She said he has connections, whatever that means."

Her temporary relief evaporated. Connections? Meaning he had friends in the professional realm and could help Eve get a new job? Or did he have criminal associations—relationships with people who could obtain lethal substances and weapons?

"Eve didn't mention his name to you? What about Dad or the others?"

"Not to me, she didn't. I'll ask your father and brothers and text you."

"I'd appreciate it. Don't forget, okay?"

"Is there something you're not telling me?"

Lindsey would've liked to unload her burdens. Her mom was a great listener and could be counted on for practical advice. It wouldn't be fair to do over the phone, from hundreds of miles away.

"Silver thought he saw her in town," she said. "I decided to check in with you."

Fortunately, her mom didn't press for more information. What could Lindsey say? *There are people who want me dead, and I think my twin sister is one of them?*

* * *

Her new phone, purchased after leaving the hospital, woke her sometime after two in the morning. Pushing on her glasses, she scooped it off the floor and eased to an upright position on the office couch. The screen indicated the caller was Eve, and she wanted to connect via video.

"Eve?"

"Lindsey." Her sister's face filled the screen. Her eyes were bloodshot, and there were dark rings underneath, but she didn't appear to be under the influence. "I want to see you."

Her heartbeat was sluggish. "Silver told me about your run-in at the hospital. How long have you been in Serenity?"

A mean-spirited snicker escaped her lips. "You should've seen his face. He was horrified, yet intrigued. You didn't show him a photo of your dear old twin?"

"Eve, what's going on? Are you here to mess with me?"

Eve had a habit of showing up in her life from time to time. She got a thrill out of shocking Lindsey's friends and coworkers and causing scenes.

Her derisive laugh had a dangerous edge to it. "Mess with you? Oh, Lindsey, I'm not interested in childish games."

Eve angled the phone, allowing her to see the vehicle and the other occupant.

She gasped. "Hedda!"

The older woman had clearly been ripped out of bed, because she was in her pajamas. No coat, no makeup. Her hair was disheveled and a gag prevented her from speaking.

Lindsey bolted to her feet, ignoring the spasm in her back. "Eve, listen to me. Silver's grandmother has nothing to do with you or me. Let her go."

Her face filled the screen again, and it was like looking at a stranger. "She won't be harmed if you follow my instructions."

"Tell me."

"Come alone to Camp Smoky, to the bluff. As soon as I see that you're alone, I'll release her."

Lindsey had no choice but to agree. Hedda was the one person in this world that Silver couldn't bear to lose.

"I'll come," she said. "Promise me you won't hurt her."

Eve laughed and ended the call. Trembling from head to toe, Lindsey shuffled to the desk and pocketed her car keys. Her coat was upstairs, but she wasn't about to alert the dogs. Getting her boots on and tied was an infuriating process. Her medication was wearing off, and her discomfort was at a thirteen on a number ten scale.

Lindsey briefly considered leaving Silver a note. She could think of only two appropriate messages—*I'm sorry* and *I love you*—neither of which he'd appreciate. He would be furious when he discovered her absence. Surely, he'd understand that she couldn't take any chances where his beloved Gram was concerned. Too many people had been hurt already. The danger could be traced back decades, to her impetuous decision to play a silly game. This was her chance to make it right. She was Eve's identical twin, after all. Lindsey was certain she could make Eve see reason.

She tiptoed into the hallway, disarmed the alarm and exited into the night. The bone-penetrating cold stole her breath. The steep concrete stairs leading up to the driveway level and her car seemed insurmountable. By the time she reached the top, she was coated in sweat and fighting nausea.

The Christmas lights were turned off inside the house. The stove hood light was on, a signal that Silver had gone to bed. Her eyes welled up, making the house blurry. Would she see him again?

Lindsey prayed the entire drive to Camp Smoky. The place was spooky in the dead of night, the murky lake a beckoning tomb, and the naked, gnarled tree branches scraped against the sky like bony fingers. Her headlights flashed over the damaged staff cabin, and her determination momentarily flagged.

Lord, help me face whatever awaits me. Put a hedge of protection around Hedda. Deliver her from danger.

She parked close to the footbridge that led to the bluff and slowly emerged. The electric pole lamp illuminated the bridge and thin stream beneath it. On the far bank, Eve stood alone with a gun in her hand and was pointing it at Lindsey.

The hard, cold truth finally sank in. Her own sister was behind the attacks on her life. Lindsey didn't have history with Miles Downing, which meant he must be doing Eve's bidding. Eve wasn't Downing's associate. She was the mastermind.

Memories of their childhood, of happy times before the fateful accident, filled her mind. Longing for innocence lost had tears dripping down her cheeks.

Grasping the railing, she stepped onto the bridge. "Hello, Eve."

TWENTY-THREE

Barking ripped Silver from a dreamless sleep. He bolted upright and was greeted by his phone buzzing and doorbell pealing. Pulling on his pants and boots, he skimmed the texts from Mason and tried to make sense of the content.

He thumped up the stairs and, after hushing Wolf and Annika, admitted his friend.

"We had a sighting of Eve," he said without preamble, brushing past Silver as he entered. "In Knoxville. A witness saw Eve and an older, silver-headed woman exiting a condo. The same condos where Hedda lives."

Silver's throat threatened to close. "When?"

"About an hour and a half ago. I came as soon as York passed on the message."

Silver's calls to Gram's landline and cell phone went unanswered. "Eve was at the hospital. She must've seen Gram, decided she'd make the perfect bait and followed her home."

Mason gestured to the windows. "Where's Lindsey's car?"

"It's not there?" Silver rushed to the door. Sure enough, her Mini Cooper wasn't in its spot. He descended the stairs at lightning speed. Mason thundered behind him.

He burst into the office and flipped the light switch.

"Gone." He thrust his fingers through his hair, disbelief coursing through him. "How did she manage to sneak out? Why didn't I hear anything?"

Mason returned to the hallway. "She must've slipped out this door."

"Eve had to have lured her out using my grandmother. No way would she have left on her own, otherwise."

Fear unlike he'd ever known seized him by the throat. This was worse than anything his father had dished out. He could handle his own suffering. But Gram and Lindsey? No way.

Mason gripped his shoulder and gave him a little shake. "Concentrate, Silver. We have to locate them quickly. Any ideas where they might've gone?"

"When Lindsey got her replacement phone yesterday, we both agreed it would be a good idea to install a locator app." He showed him the screen. "According to this, they're at Camp Smoky."

"Makes sense. Eve's comfortable there, since she's orchestrated several attempts on Lindsey. Knows the property. How do you want to play this?"

"If we call in the cavalry, we risk something going wrong. Eve is obviously unhinged." Already returning to his bedroom for his gun, he said over his shoulder, "Contact Cruz and Raven."

As they navigated the deserted, winding roads in Mason's truck, he wished he had his Corvette. He could've made the trip in half the time.

Impatience ate at him. What if they were too late? What if they got there and discovered the worst had happened?

He thumped his fist against his leg, frustration boiling over. "Why did she walk into danger alone?"

"She's got to be reeling right now. Think about it—her

own sister." Mason emitted a grunt of disgust. "How would you feel if you were in her shoes?"

Lindsey had carried the weight of responsibility since the day Thea had received an arrow in her place. Learning that her own sister was behind the violence had devastated her. He'd seen her wilt from the inside out like a water-parched flower, seen the grief written plainly on her face. She would go to great lengths to stop Eve from hurting someone else.

They left the truck at the camp entrance and hiked in. There wasn't time to wait on Raven and Cruz and concoct a plan. The sight of Lindsey's car sent an arrow of trepidation through him. She wasn't in any condition to face off against anyone.

As they neared the footbridge, they heard talking near the bluff's edge. Beyond the bridge, the rocky overlook was draped mostly in shadows. Eve was standing with Gram beside the waist-high barrier, the only thing between her and a drop to the valley floor miles below. She had a gun wedged in Gram's ribs. Lindsey stood facing them, arms outstretched, palms up in entreaty. He couldn't make out her words, but he could see her desperation.

Flames of fury seethed inside him. At Mason's cue, they separated and approached the shallow stream from opposite sides of the bridge, staying beyond the reaches of light. His weapon drawn, he entered the icy stream and moved at a snail's pace to avoid splashes. At the other side, he crawled on his belly up the bank.

"You promised to let her go," Lindsey said, her voice wobbly. "She's done nothing wrong."

"I will as soon as you're out of the way."

Silver lifted up on his elbow and saw Eve motion with her gun. "Climb over the barrier."

Lindsey turned her head and contemplated the vast emptiness. On the other side of the rock barrier, there were a series of ledges that jutted out over the treetops. Beyond that, nothing but open sky.

"I understand why you're upset." Lindsey inched her way to the barrier. "I shouldn't have pressured you into that game."

"Upset?" she scoffed. "Don't you mean miserable? Infuriated? You were always the instigator. Why weren't *you* the one who slipped and crashed into that table? It's not fair!"

The identical twins couldn't have been more different; one radiated goodness and hope and the other despair and hatred.

"I'm sorry, Eve."

"Save it. You don't know what it's like to have people recoil when they see you. Kids gasp and point. Sometimes they run to their mommies in fright. Sometimes people say nasty things to my face."

"I tried to shield you from that when we were younger. To protect you."

"You think I wanted anything to do with you?" she demanded. "Every time I look at you, I see what I lost. I see the life I should've had. You robbed me of a normal life, Lindsey."

"You could've had a good life, you know," Lindsey shot back, angry now. "You were determined to marinate in your self-pity."

"Shut up."

"All those years, we were too busy feeling sorry for you to speak the truth. We let you become entrenched in your anger, regret and bitterness. You've gone too far. This is *murder*, Eve. You'll get caught. You'll spend the rest of your life behind bars."

"I'm already in a prison of your making," she bit out.

"Did Miles plant this idea of revenge? Did he talk you into coming after me?"

"Like I needed anyone for that. I've been dreaming about payback for a very long time. Miles was the key. He opened doors for me. Introduced me to the right people."

"So it was you who shot Thea?" Lindsey demanded. "Who hunted me down like prey?"

"I fell in with a group of avid hunters a couple years ago and took to the bow and arrow like a duck to water."

Eve's self-satisfaction grated on Silver's stretched-thin patience. She was proud of her deadly skills.

"I told Miles what I wanted, and he supplied the toxin. He offered to do the deed himself, but I wanted the satisfaction."

"I don't understand how you could stand over me, your own twin, and watch me suffer."

Eve's face screwed into spite, and her eyes spit nails. "Of course, you don't." She jabbed her finger at the barrier. "Climb over. No one will find your body. Even if they do, you won't be recognizable."

"Think about Mom and Dad. Our brothers."

"Do as I say, or watch me put a bullet in your boyfriend's grandmother."

Silver looked past the bridge and met Mason's gaze. They'd reached the point of no return. At his nod, they leaped up, trained their weapons on the target and announced their presence.

Eve pointed her gun at Hedda. Lindsey cried out and lunged forward, tackling her sister and propelling her to the ground.

Mason raced to shield Hedda while the sisters rolled into the grass. In no time, Eve had Lindsey pinned to the ground, the barrel of her gun flush with her forehead.

Silver knew in that moment that he would trade places

with her in a heartbeat. Not because she was a skilled assistant or a kind, generous person. Not because she was a loyal friend. But because he wanted to spend every day with her for the rest of his life.

Forgive me, Lindsey.

He called out, startling Eve. He capitalized on her distraction by putting a bullet through her. She howled, slumped over on her side and pointed her gun at him.

"Don't," he growled, hurriedly pressing his boot on her wrist to hold her in place.

Blood spilled from a wound in her upper right chest. As soon as he'd pried her gun from her fingers and handed it off to Mason, his gaze sought Lindsey's.

"You okay?"

She nodded, lying there in the grass looking stunned. "Hedda?"

Gram's gag had been removed. She walked toward them unassisted, enveloped in Mason's coat. "I'm fine."

Mason got handcuffs on Eve and inspected her wound. "Probably need surgery, but you should make it."

Rage turned her gaze black, and she scowled at them.

Silver rubbed Gram's back. "You sure you're okay?"

"Right as rain." Strength and vitality shone from her eyes.

Reassured, he crouched beside Lindsey and cupped her cold cheek. "You can lie here as long as you need. Catch your breath."

Her lower lip trembled. She reached for him. "Oh, Silver…"

He slid his arm beneath her shoulders and helped her sit up. She slumped against him, curling her fingers into his shirt and holding on tightly—as if he planned to let her go anytime soon. His heart was full. There was so much he needed to say to her, but not here. Not now.

Silver didn't get a chance to be alone with her for hours. Cruz and Raven reached the camp as paramedics were loading Eve into an ambulance. Detective York met them at the hospital and took their statements. After Gram had been checked and pronounced healthy, Mason offered to take her home. Silver had stayed by Lindsey's side while she spoke with her parents and explained everything that had happened. Her tears had nearly broken him. She and her family had a tough road ahead. He was determined to be a source of support, if she'd let him.

Eve had come through surgery without complications and was projected to make a full recovery. As soon as she was able, she would face the consequences of her actions. Miles Downing had started talking as soon as he'd heard his cohort was in custody. Eve had perpetrated most of the attacks alone—she'd pursued them at the camp on foot and again in the heavy-duty truck. When those attempts failed, she'd talked Miles into helping and eventually found an ally in Tyson. The security guard had gambling debts that the money—coughed up by Miles—would erase. Eve had drawn them into her web of insanity, and they would pay the price.

It was after dawn when Silver got Lindsey home. "I guess you're ready to sleep?"

She eased onto the couch and stared at the twinkling tree. "I don't think I can. Not yet."

Silver settled on the cushion and angled his body toward her. "What happens now?"

Behind the glasses, her brown eyes widened. "It's over, isn't it? I mean, there will be hearings and court dates. The danger is over, though."

"You can do whatever you want."

"I don't know that I want to continue at the camp."

"Eugene will understand."

A dip formed between her brows. "I'm not sure what I would do in Serenity for work, though."

He smiled. "Aren't you?"

Her gaze searched his for long moments. Then her lips parted. What did she see? How much he adored her?

Silver trailed his fingertips along her jawline and took her chin between this thumb and forefinger. "I know this is terrible timing, but I have to tell you something."

"Yes?"

"I want you to stay in Serenity."

"You want me to work for you again?"

"That's not exactly what I meant." His midsection was a jumble of nerves. "Believe me, I'd like nothing more than for you to resume your position at Hearthside Rentals. It's more important to me that you stick around for personal reasons."

Her breath caught. "It is?"

He lowered his lips to hers and pressed a lingering kiss there. His heart threatened to explode. "I love you, Lindsey," he murmured against her mouth.

She framed his face with her hands, urging him to lift his head and meet her wonder-filled gaze. "You love me? Truly?"

"I do."

"You're sure?"

"No question. No doubt. I love you, Lindsey Snow."

"But what I did…can you truly overcome it?"

"I already have. I've forgiven you, Lindsey. It took almost losing you to snap me out of my self-pity. I understand why you agreed to my parents' request, and I know why you ultimately couldn't continue, why you had to quit working for me."

"I couldn't continue to deceive you because I cared about you." Her eyes sparkled to rival the brightest Christmas tree. "I love you," she said shyly. "I've loved you for a long time."

Joy and contentment took root in his heart. He was amazed at how God had used disastrous circumstances to bring a priceless gift into his life—an unforeseen love, a relationship to nourish and cherish, a forever partner.

EPILOGUE

Christmas Eve

Silver was at the door before she could ring the bell. His smile—the one reserved just for her—dazzled her. Around him, she tended to forget everything else.

His violet gaze shimmered with affection. When he took in her fitted red dress, purchased especially for this Christmas Eve dinner, longing mingled with admiration.

"You are stunning," he murmured, draping her coat on the couch.

Her cheeks heated. His compliments made her blush. When he slid his hand beneath her hair, cupped her nape and brought his impossibly handsome face close, she swayed toward him, eager for his kiss. He didn't disappoint. His lips were firm, sure and gentle.

When he lifted his head, there was a flash of uncertainty, a glimpse of nerves, and she wondered at it. "I've missed you," he murmured.

Lindsey grinned. "I've seen you every day."

Sunday morning, she'd moved into Raven's house until she could find a suitable apartment. She'd decided to return to Hearthside Rentals. After explaining to Eugene that Camp Smoky held too many bad memories, she'd promised to ease the transition of whoever replaced her. He'd had a long conversation with Bruce and Kayla, and they'd finally agreed to honor his wishes.

Lindsey was happy to resume her work with the cabins. Thea had warned that romance might complicate matters, but Lindsey didn't share those reservations. If anything, they were more effective as a cohesive team.

He took her hand. "Did you speak with Eve today?"

"She's refusing visitors still."

A pang of sadness gripped her...for herself, true, but mostly for Eve. She could've had a very different future.

"Your parents haven't seen her yet?"

She shook her head. Her parents had driven to Serenity the day after the confrontation at the bluff. Silver had supported her through that difficult conversation. "They're heartbroken."

Silver's brow furrowed. "Your dad seems shattered. I can't imagine."

"It's going to take time and lots of prayer." She squeezed his hand. "You're the one bright spot in all of this."

He looked startled. "Me?"

"You risked your life to keep me safe. That makes you pretty special in their eyes." She smiled. "You're also the man I'm madly in love with."

His gaze heating, he lifted her hand and brushed a kiss on her knuckles. "I'm pretty fond of you, too."

"I got you a present," she said. "I know it's tradition to wait until Christmas Day, but I'm hoping you'll open it now."

He followed her into the living room and watched as she selected a large, heavy present from behind the tree.

"When did you put this here?" Silver said, coming to help. "Let me. You shouldn't strain your back."

"While you were at the stables yesterday. My dad carried it inside." Her lower back had turned appalling shades of purple and yellow. She would have to continue to take pain reliever for a few more days, but she was more mobile than she had been. Her leg wound was also healing.

Silver placed the present on the coffee table and, taking a seat, patted the cushion next to him. Lindsey bit her lip as he removed the foil paper. He examined the curio cabinet, running his fingers along the polished cherry and inspecting the slots.

"It's for the keepsakes your nanny gave you," she said, hoping she'd gotten this right.

His expression was somber. Beyond that, she couldn't guess his thoughts.

"You wouldn't have to put it in a high-traffic space. You could keep it in your bedroom."

His eyes looked shiny. "It's perfect, Lindsey. Truly. Keeping Ruth's gifts hidden away doesn't honor her. Would you mind helping me choose a spot for this later?"

"I'd be happy to."

"I was thinking… I'd like to pay her a visit after the holidays. Would you come with me?"

"If my boss agrees to give me time off, I will."

He grinned. "That could probably be arranged. I'll put in a good word for you."

"Have you heard from your parents?" The news of one twin trying to kill the other had popped up across social media sites, and Lindsey had been dodging news reporters for days. They surely would've seen the articles.

The question didn't evoke anger, only resignation. "I reached out to them and explained that if they interfere in my life again, my silence will no longer be guaranteed."

Lindsey understood why he didn't want to expose his experience to public scrutiny. Fortunately, he had decided to work through the past with a trusted counselor.

"I also warned them not to speak to the media about you, should anyone come snooping around."

"Gordon and Astrid know we're together?"

He nodded, his gaze soaking her in. "That's one thing they got right." He kissed her, took her hands and urged her up. "I have something to show you."

He led her into the dining room, which was aglow with candles.

"What's this?" Lindsey walked around the table. Dozens of gingerbread cookies were laid out on platters, waiting to be decorated. There was a rainbow display of candy toppings and tubes of icing.

"I thought you might like to help me decorate these and dole them out to our cabin guests. There are enough for Serenity's first responders, as well."

"I'd love to." They'd done this last year together, and it was one of her fondest memories.

"Just so you know, I didn't make these. I ordered them from the bakery."

She snagged one and bit off a hand. "They're much better than mine."

He wrapped his fingers around her wrist, bent his head and bit off the other hand. "I have to disagree. You're as skilled in the kitchen as you are in the office."

"I don't know about that." She laughed.

Silver reached for a white box and handed it to her. "I, uh, bought one already decorated. I thought we could use it as a template…"

Lindsey opened the lid and stared at the intricate piping on the gingerbread man. He was wearing a Christmassy suit in greens and reds, and he had gray hair and violet eyes. In one hand was an icing rose bouquet. In the other, he was holding something small and round. Surely that wasn't what she thought it was…

She looked up to find Silver holding a bouquet of roses and a velvet box. He went down on one knee, cleared his throat and smiled up at her. "I love you, Lindsey. I've discovered I can't live without you."

Lindsey's jaw dropped. "You're serious? You want to marry me?"

He put the roses down and opened the box. A tasteful, beautiful diamond ring winked against the dark fabric.

This was real. Silver was proposing marriage. A lifetime together. Before she committed, she had to be 100 percent certain he wouldn't have regrets.

"What about your parents? What I did? And Eve? She almost killed your grandmother."

"She almost killed the love of my life, too," he said, his gaze unfaltering. "And I shot her for it." He stood and took her hand, pressing her fingers between his. "We've overcome many obstacles to get to this point, haven't we? None of that is enough to keep us apart." His love for her was written on his face—fixed, unmovable, unchanging. "But if you have reservations, if it's too soon, I'll wait. I'll wait for as long as I have to because you're worth it. And my love isn't going to fade or diminish. That I can promise you."

Lindsey held out her left hand in invitation. "It's not too soon. I have *zero* reservations, because I love you, Silver. I simply had to be sure you didn't before I said yes."

His mouth curved into a beaming, blinding grin. He slid the ring onto her finger and gazed deeply into her eyes. "I think life with you is going to be an adventure, Lindsey Snow."

She slid her arms around his waist and grinned up at him. "One thing's for sure. You'll never have a dull or lonely Christmas ever again."

* * * * *

Dear Reader,

Are you as enthusiastic about Christmas as Lindsey Snow? I grew to admire her character during the course of this story. Despite her poor decisions in the past and stark circumstances in the present, she didn't lose her optimism or hope. Her faith didn't falter, either. I'm a big fan of her and Silver together, and I hope you are, too.

Like Eve and Silver, we all experience trials in life. We handle them differently, though, don't we? The key is to take our burdens to Jesus and allow Him to heal us. He's able and willing to see us through the valleys, and He'll celebrate with us on the mountaintops! My prayer for you, dear reader, is that you would enjoy a close, personal relationship with Him. God's Word will point you in the right direction.

Merry Christmas and God Bless,
Karen Kirst

COMING NEXT MONTH FROM
Love Inspired Suspense

BLIZZARD SHOWDOWN
Alaska K-9 Unit • by Shirlee McCoy
After months of searching for Violet James, Gabriel Runyon and his K-9 partner finally track her down—just in time to rescue her from her ex-fiancé. Now it's up to them to safeguard the single mother and her newborn daughter. But can they outrun a blizzard *and* an enemy who wants Violet dead?

CHRISTMAS K-9 PROTECTORS
Alaska K-9 Unit • by Lenora Worth and Maggie K. Black
Members of the K-9 team face danger and find love in these holiday novellas, in which a rookie K-9 trooper and his furry partner must save a forensic scientist from a ruthless jewelry thief, and a tech whiz, a criminal psychologist and a K-9 go on the run to keep a teen out of the hands of a kidnapping gang.

AMISH CHRISTMAS ESCAPE
Amish Country Justice • by Dana R. Lynn
In the sights of a murderer, Christy O'Malley knows there is just one person she can rely on to shield her—her estranged husband, who doesn't know he is a father. But when she shows up on Sam Burkholder's doorstep in Amish country, can he help her and their little girl live through Christmas?

CHRISTMAS VENDETTA
Emergency Responders • by Valerie Hansen
Teacher Sandy Lynn Forrester's peaceful Christmas vacation is interrupted when somebody tries to kill her—but the cops don't think the threat is real. The only person who believes her is a man she doesn't trust: framed and discredited cop Clay Danforth. But with her life on the line, he's her best chance at survival...

CAPTURED AT CHRISTMAS
by Jodie Bailey
Undercover with an infantry unit to investigate the theft of hard drives, military investigator Captain Rachel Blake doesn't expect the holiday assignment to turn into a protection mission. But when Captain Marshall Slater and his little girl are targeted, she'll risk everything to help keep them safe.

WYOMING CHRISTMAS PERIL
by Kathie Ridings
Fleeing from a murderous bank robber at Christmastime, Bailey O'Keefe has only FBI agent Sean Hanson to protect her. But when their safe house is breached, can Bailey and Sean outmaneuver their enemy while battling the elements and the hazards of the snow-packed trails on Cougar Mountain?

LISCNM1121